NEW BEGIN AT THE FARM ON MUDDYPUDDLE LANE

Heart-warming, uplifting romance

Etti Summers

CHAPTER ONE

Dulcie Fairfax nearly squealed with excitement as she drove along the quaintest little high street she had ever seen. Picklewick was a gorgeous village, and she was so excited to think that she would soon be living here.

Actually, she wouldn't be living in the village as such, but just outside, on a farm. How much outside she had yet to determine, but she didn't think it would be very far. She had Google-mapped it of course, just to check the distance, but looking online wasn't the same as seeing it in person, was it? And driving wouldn't be the same as walking. She dearly hoped the farm would be close enough for her to be able to walk into the village. She didn't want to have to drive everywhere, and neither would she be able to afford a taxi if she wanted to pop down to the little village pub for a drink of an evening.

Ah, there it was, The Black Horse. The pub looked even cuter in real life than it had on the internet and if she hadn't had her hands firmly clamped on the wheel of her recently-purchased mint green Fiat 500, she would have clapped them in excitement. She couldn't wait to get to know the locals – her fellow villagers, she amended hastily, because as of this morning she **was** a local.

It was a hard thing to get her head around.

Yesterday she had been living in Birmingham, in a rented flat: today she would be living in Picklewick in her very own home.

Dulcie let out an excited giggle, still not able to believe her luck. In fact, she probably wouldn't believe it was real until she had the keys in her hand, and even then she might have to pinch herself a few times. She didn't see why the solicitor who had done the conveyancing couldn't have given her the keys when she had signed the contract this morning, but he had informed her that the previous owner was insisting on meeting her at the property to hand the keys over in person, so it looked like she would have to wait to get her mitts on them.

To be honest, she could have done without meeting the guy. She just wanted to move in and savour the knowledge that she was now a property owner. Her,

Dulcie Fairfax, who had never owned so much as a dolls house, was now the proud owner of Lilac Tree Farm. All thirty-seven acres of it – whatever an acre was.

Technically, she knew how big that was – she had read that it was the equivalent of sixteen tennis courts, but that information didn't help in the slightest. Neither did seeing a copy of the deeds with the farm's boundary highlighted. She simply couldn't envisage its size.

As per directions, Dulcie drove through the village, rather more slowly than she would have normally done because she was too busy trying to glance at the shops to either side of the street. Soon though, she had left the last house behind, and almost immediately, the vista opened up to reveal fields, and above them rolling hillsides. Everything was startlingly green and incredibly lush, and she wound the window down and took a deep breath of amazingly fresh air. She was reminded of the camping holidays her family used to go on as a child, although that was usually to the seaside and not to the heart of rural England. And this was quite rural indeed – far more rural than she was anticipating, she thought as she glanced in her rear view mirror to see how far she had travelled from the village.

To her consternation, all she could see of Picklewick was the square turret of the church in the distance, and she swiftly dragged her eyes back to the road ahead, feeling out of her comfort zone. It was all well and good visiting a place like Picklewick for a weekend break and marvelling at how lovely it was to get away from it all, but she suspected it was another thing entirely to live here, and a worm of unease squirmed in her tummy.

As she continued to drive along the B road leading out of the village, she kept her eyes peeled for a turn-off on her right-hand side, and when she spotted the sign for Muddypuddle Lane she slowed down and drank in her surroundings as she made the turn. The lane was a roughly tarmacked track leading up the hillside, and in the murky distance she could see a cluster of buildings on the right, which she assumed was the riding stables she had noticed on Google. To further backup her assumption, horses grazed in the fields on either side of the lane and a faint animal aroma wafted up her nose through the car's open window.

For a moment she panicked, as it suddenly occurred to her that there might be animals on the farm. Big ones, like sheep and cows. But then she remembered that the contract thankfully hadn't included any livestock. She owned the house, the barns and all the outbuildings, and thirty-seven acres of land which was mostly pasture, plus a small woodland, an orchard and a stream. Oh, and the farm also came with grazing rights on the hillside above. Not that she would ever use those rights, but it was nice to know she had them, just in case.

The hillside couldn't be seen at the moment as it was encased in mist, and neither could she see a farmhouse. Everything above the stables was invisible, and once more her stomach turned over with worry. Was there really a farm up there, or had this whole thing been a huge hoax? That someone might be playing a nasty trick on her passed through her mind, and she scanned the surrounding fields, wondering if a camera crew was going to jump out at her and record her horrified reaction for the whole world to see. Or worse – someone might be luring her to a grisly end!

Passing the stables (the animal smell was more pronounced here and she promptly wound her window back up) she glanced over at it and was relieved to see people leading horses across the yard. If she was about to be done away with, there was a chance someone might hear her screams.

Debating whether it would be prudent to cut her losses, turn around and go home, she was about to do just that – even though she had given up her flat, so didn't have a home to go back to – when she saw the shadow of a building up ahead on the left. Drawing closer, the building became a cottage, with a light shining in one of the downstairs rooms, and in the distance, on the opposite side of the lane, several more buildings hoved into view.

Dulcie's heart fluttered when she saw a worn and battered wooden sign that said Lilac Tree Farm, and she realised that she had finally reached her destination. Her former worries were shoved to the back of her mind as excitement surged through her once more. This was it! She was finally going to see what she had won!

She hadn't been able to believe her luck when she had opened the email informing her that she had won a dream farmhouse in the country, and she'd had to read it several times and had even forwarded it to her whole family for their opinion, before she had tentatively conceded that maybe, just maybe, she had actually **won** something. Dulcie never won anything. Ever. No matter what she entered – from a raffle in her sister Nikki's school summer fete, to a giveaway on social media – she had never won anything. Until she had won this farm.

She had entered the raffle (or was it a lottery? – she hadn't been too sure) out of sheer desperation. Her family, her brother Jay especially, used to tease her for entering so many competitions, but who was doing the teasing now, eh? She was! Not that she was crowing about it, but she did feel quietly smug. Her life was about to change dramatically and for the better, and all because she had purchased a ticket to win a farm.

Of course, she would have to carry on with her boring job for the time being because she still had bills to pay, but a bright new future beckoned and a more exciting life in the country lay ahead.

After the news had sunk in and she had checked that it wasn't a scam, Dulcie had spent all her free time between then and now pinning images to Pinterest and building board after board of lovely things. Things such as kitchen accessories for all the jam-making, baking and pickling that she intended to do; old-fashioned metal bedsteads and nightstands with china jugs on them; real fires and Aga ranges with baby lambs in boxes keeping warm in front of them.

Okay, maybe she would give the lambs a miss, because she wasn't too keen on sheep. The closest she'd got to one was petting a woolly head as it had tried to butt her during a visit to a city farm when she was a child. Dulcie had studiously avoided the creatures since, which hadn't been difficult considering that sheep were few and far between in the Bournville area of Birmingham where she had lived until yesterday.

The car juddered into a pothole the size of a moon crater, and Dulcie swore under her breath. This lane was badly pitted and she was forced to haul the steering wheel from side to side to avoid them, just when she wanted to concentrate on the farm up ahead.

She hoped it had a thatched roof. From the photo advertising the raffle, it had been difficult to tell. The focus had been on a large planter that had once been a stone trough of some kind but was now reincarnated as a flowerpot. A ginger cat had been sitting in front of it, washing its paws, and a bottle of milk (a real glass bottle with a metal stoppered top, would you believe!) stood next to it. The farmhouse had been a soft blur in the background, but she had been able to make out a grey-coloured stone building and sunlight glinting off the windows. There had been several arty photos of the interior – beams, flagstone floors, vintage hand-painted tiles framing an open fireplace, and quaint wooden cupboards. It had looked idyllic.

A house like that would surely have climbing roses growing around the door, and a wood pile for the fire that she would light in the winter. She knew her property had a stream running through it, an orchard and meadows, and she imagined dancing barefoot through the grass, trailing her hands along the tops of the stems, sunlight casting a golden glow over everything. She would be wearing a white flowing dress and have flowers woven through her hair, and—

'You've got to be kidding me!' Dulcie slammed her foot on the break and the car skidded to an untidy halt. Her eyes widened and her stomach did a nasty forward roll as she took in the scene in front of her.

There was no thatch. There were no roses climbing up the walls. There **was** a stone trough though, she saw, having almost collided with it, but it didn't contain the riotous tumbling mass of flowers she had expected. The plants were limp and lifeless, and hadn't been watered for some time. There was no sign of the cat, either.

The house itself was built out of grey stone and had a grey slate roof. The front door had a little v-shaped porch over the top of it with a window to either side, and there were three further windows on the top floor. The farmhouse looked boxy and solid, and not the least bit how she had imagined it. She knew that the blurb had said the house was rustic, but there was rustic and there was run-down. If she didn't know better, she would have said that the place was derelict.

However, there was a large black SUV sitting menacingly in the middle of the yard, looking totally out of place, and leaning against its bonnet with his legs crossed and his arms folded, was one of the most attractive men Dulcie had ever seen.

Otto York heard the rumble of an engine coming up the pitted track long before the vehicle came into view, and for a moment he thought it might turn into the stables. But when it kept on coming, he nodded. This must be the new owner, and although he was curious who this unknown woman might be, he wasn't looking forward to handing the keys over, because that would mean the end of his family living and working on Lilac Tree Farm.

It was the end of an era, and it saddened him immensely.

He blamed himself. He was the last of the Yorks, apart from his father, Walter, and he should have taken more interest in it. Selfishly, he hadn't given the future of the farm a second thought when he had buggered off to catering college seventeen years ago, and he hadn't given it a great deal of thought since. Too busy following his dream of becoming a top-notch chef, he had immersed himself in all things culinary and had ignored the farm.

His dad had always seemed so capable and strong. Although his father was in his seventies, Otto had stupidly assumed he would go on forever. Even when Mum had passed away, his dad had carried on stalwartly, and although Otto knew he missed her dreadfully, his dad had continued to work the farm as he had always done.

Otto grunted as the engine noise faltered for a second, and he guessed the vehicle must have hit one of the many potholes which cratered the lane. Nathan, the general manager of the stables down the road, had been promising to re-tarmac it for some time, but hadn't got around to it. Otto wondered whether he should offer to lend a hand, to get the ball rolling so to speak, because how else would he occupy his days now that the sheep had been sold (apart from Flossie, who Dad hadn't been able to part with) and the farm had a new owner as from this morning.

He also supposed he should try to get a job, since it didn't look like he'd be returning to London and his position as head chef in one of the best restaurants in the city anytime soon. How could he when his father needed him here?

If Otto was truthful, his dad had needed him here years ago, but Walter had been too proud and too stubborn to admit it. Otto was forced to admit that his father had been struggling for a long time, but Otto had selfishly refused to see it.

Good lord! Otto screwed up his eyes as he squinted at the car emerging out of the mist. A green Fiat 500 bounced into view, its suspension handling the uneven surface of the cobbled farmyard with a jauntiness which wasn't reflected on the face of its driver, whose eyes were wide and whose mouth was in the shape of an O as it skidded to a stop.

The woman didn't look at all pleased, and she looked even more unhappy when it began to rain just as she cut the engine and got out, the mist turning into the kind of drizzle that didn't seem to warrant an umbrella but soaked you all the same.

He watched her glance skywards and frown. Then her eyes met his and he was shaken to his core.

She was bloody gorgeous. He guessed her to be in her late twenties, slim yet curvaceous, with a face a model would envy – and he'd seen enough of those in his time, although why anyone wanted to come to his restaurant simply to pick at his food was beyond him.

Okay, maybe not model material, because she was no stick-insect and she didn't have that haughty air models seemed to cultivate, and neither did she have the razor-sharp cheekbones; but she did have glossy dark hair that bounced on blazer-clad shoulders, a flowy white top that failed to hide her figure, and long legs encased in a pair of skinny jeans which ended in impossibly high heels.

His gaze was drawn to them as he wondered how the hell she was going to walk across muddy cobbles wearing those, before creeping up her body to reach her face again.

Her eyes had narrowed and the set of her lips told him that she'd clocked him checking her out.

It wasn't something he usually did when he met a woman for the first time, and it put him on the back foot. So he did the only thing he could think of. He narrowed his own eyes, hardened his jaw, and waited for her to come to him.

She tottered towards him on those ridiculous heels, and he was about to introduce himself when she stumbled and uttered an ear-piercing shriek as a hen fluttered out from underneath his car, squawking loudly.

His hand shot out to catch her and he gripped the woman's arm firmly, not wanting her to face-plant the cobbles.

She wobbled precariously for a heartbeat, before finding her balance.

But when the hen clucked and strutted around her feet, the woman let out another shriek and flapped a hand at it.

'Shoo! Go away! Get lost!' she cried, hopping from foot to foot like an ungainly stork, as the hen, oblivious to the ructions it was causing, tried to peck at the shiny gold buckles on her ankle straps. 'Make it go away,' she pleaded. 'It's attacking me.'

'It's not. She's hoping you've got food for her.'

'Well, I haven't. So there,' she added.

Otto took pity on her. He released his grip on her arm, hoping she wouldn't fall over, and clapped his hands a couple of times.

The hen took the hint and scuttled off into one of the barns, probably to join the other hens who still resided at the farm. By rights he should have sold them off, but they had been overlooked in his haste to sort everything else out.

'Better?' he asked, somewhat sarcastically. Lilac Tree Farm's new owner might be as attractive as hell, but she was no farmer. Everything about her, from her cute little run-around to her four-inch heels, screamed city girl. Of all the people who could have won the farm, why did it have to be someone who didn't have a clue what they were doing?

Good luck, he thought. She was going to need it.

With a loud sigh, he said, 'Am I right in assuming you're Dulcie Fairfax?'

'Yes. What is that chicken doing here?'

'What did you expect? This **is** a farm.'

She glared at him. 'Are there anymore?'

'Another two.' He took a breath and bit back his sarcastic reply. After all, he had stressed to the solicitor that the farm would be transferred to the new owner without livestock, so maybe he was being harsh. Perhaps he was doing her an injustice, and the hen scurrying out from underneath his car had simply startled her.

In an attempt to appear more friendly, although all he felt was sadness and resentment that a stranger was going to be living on the farm where he had grown up, he said, 'I hope you'll be happy in your new home,' and held out a bunch of keys.

Warily, she took them from him, her gaze scouring his face. 'Thanks.'

Otto hesitated for a moment, wondering whether he should say something more profound, like 'take care of it', then he grunted at his stupidity. The farm belonged to Dulcie now. It was up to her whether she made a go of it or not. It was no longer any concern of his.

CHAPTER TWO

Dulcie hurried to unlock the door to the farmhouse, anxious to go inside.

Her reason was fourfold. First, she wanted to make sure that these really were the keys to her new home and that the man in the yard wasn't some psycho who had lured her here under false pretences: which reminded her – she must get all the locks changed as soon as possible. Second, she wanted to get out of this annoying rain. Third, she was desperate to see inside the house; and last, but not least (**definitely** not least) she wanted to escape from the gaze of her farm's former owner.

 She couldn't believe the way Walter York had looked her up and down with a scornful sneer on his face. She knew his name because it had appeared on the contract – and just for the record, it didn't suit him, she decided. And the way he'd behaved when she had been startled by that blasted chicken had been downright mean. There had been no need for him to be so sarcastic about it. Even though in her daydreams about the farm she might have envisioned collecting fresh eggs every morning, call her naive but she hadn't expected a close encounter with the creature that actually produced those eggs.

He could have been a bit more welcoming, she thought. Then she decided it didn't matter. It was unlikely their paths would cross in the future, and if she never saw him again, it would be too soon. Talk about being unfriendly. He had taken grumpiness to a whole new level.

Which made her wonder why he had insisted on meeting her in the first place. He could just as easily have left the keys with the solicitor for her to collect when she signed the contract, so she suspected that the real reason he'd wanted to hand them over in person was to check out the new owner.

What a jerk!

She was glad she'd met him though, if only so she knew to avoid him in future. She certainly wouldn't forget his face in a hurry. Good looking didn't begin to describe him, but he knew it. Haughty, arrogant... there were probably a few other choice words she could think of, and as she was mulling them over another one popped into her head – **disturbing**.

But she wasn't entirely sure why – unless it was the incongruity of the state of the farm, compared to his appearance.

Dulcie had noticed how well-dressed he was. He looked like an image of how she thought a gentleman farmer should look, and she wondered why he had raffled the farm off instead of selling it. She was aware that all proceeds were going to charity, so perhaps he had hoped to raise more money this way, which was extremely altruistic of him and she had to admire him for that, but she was also envious that he was wealthy enough to be able to afford to make such a grand gesture.

He certainly appeared to be well off, what with that car and those clothes. And the stuck-up attitude was very lord-of-the-manor, leading her to wonder if he actually did live in a mansion. He was also well-spoken, his voice crisp and clipped, with no discernible accent. She had a feeling he was used to barking out orders.

From the doorstep Dulcie watched his car glide out of the yard, irritation gnawing at her. Trust his car to **glide,** when hers had juddered and jarred over those blasted cobbles. She didn't think her poor car's suspension would ever recover and she hoped she hadn't done it any permanent damage.

The SUV's tail lights disappeared around the corner, and suddenly the world became all the murkier for their departure as Dulcie abruptly realised that she was on her own, in the middle of nowhere, with only a chicken for company.

Dear god, what had she let herself in for, she wondered, as she backed inside the house and firmly closed the door.

Then she turned around to see what her new home had to offer – and immediately wished she hadn't.

She was standing in a dingy hall whose dominant colour was beigey-brown, with a worryingly steep and narrow staircase at the far end. There were two doors leading off the hall, one to either side, and Dulcie tentatively pushed open the one to her left to reveal a sitting room containing a pair of wing-backed leather armchairs that had seen better days. The thought of sitting on the cracked and scratched cushions made her shudder.

Still, they looked clean enough, as did the rest of the room. It was just a pity everything was so worn and old-fashioned. She quite liked the fireplace, though. A chunky black stove was recessed into the chimney breast and a pile of chopped wood was stacked neatly by the side, and she remembered the tiles surrounding it from the photos when she'd bought a ticket.

Two of the walls were whitewashed stone, and heavy beams stretched across the ceiling. It would have been quaint if it wasn't for the woodchip wallpaper, the stern grey flagstone floor (which wasn't quite as appealing in real life) and the heavy burgundy curtains.

A door was directly ahead, and Dulcie walked towards it, her eyes darting here and there as she entered a kitchen, taking everything in.

Her heart sank again. She hadn't been expecting anything ultra-modern and sleek, but she had at least been hoping for farmhouse style. This kitchen was more **rubbish-tip** style: the whole thing needed ripping out and replacing.

Trying to look on the positive side and not give in to the tears that were threatening, Dulcie told herself that the room was a lovely size, and that the tatty stand-alone dresser and assorted cupboards would do for now, until she could afford to replace them with a proper fitted kitchen. If she ever could afford to replace it, that is, because on her meagre wage she would be lucky if she could even cover the day-to-day running costs of a property this size.

Dulcie bit her lip to hold back a wail. She had been so looking forward to living here and so excited about her brand-new life in the country, that the run-down reality of what she had won made her want to cry. Perhaps she should cut her losses now, put it on the market and get rid of it? With the proceeds from the sale, she would have enough money to buy something nice. Something more modern, that wasn't in the middle of nowhere. How much was a place like this worth anyway, she mused. Dulcie couldn't begin to guess, but surely she would get a fair bit for it if she sold it?

Telling herself not to be too hasty and that she shouldn't make any knee-jerk decisions, she explored the rest of the house.

The kitchen had a walk-in pantry, the shelves stripped bare, but in her mind's eye she could imagine jars of pickles and preserves lining them, and for the first time since she had driven into the muddy farmyard, a flicker of excitement ignited in her stomach.

Perhaps she was being unrealistic to have expected her farmhouse to look anything like those gorgeous images she had on her Pinterest board. And although her house was a far cry from how she had imagined it, at least it was **hers.** And to put an even more positive spin on things, she told herself that this was a blank canvas, to decorate and design as the mood took her.

Just off the kitchen was a utility room – at least, that was what she would use it for. At the moment all it contained was a row of pegs on the wall and a bucket in the corner. It had a door to the outside though, so it would be a perfect place in which to hang coats and leave wet boots to dry.

Dulcie peered through the small window to the side of the door, noticing that the glass was clean, and she wondered whether Walter York had given the place a once over with a duster before relinquishing the keys. She doubted it somehow. He didn't strike her as the type to get his hands dirty; he probably had staff to do that for him.

A garden lay to the rear of the house, although it was seriously overgrown, and a path ran through the middle of it, disappearing into the mist. Another frisson of excitement travelled through her as she wondered where it led, but exploring the outside would have to wait. She wanted to see the upstairs first. Anyway it was raining, and her umbrella was buried in one of the boxes in the back of her hatchback.

The utility room had a second door and she opened it cautiously, hoping it didn't lead to a cellar. Dulcie wasn't keen on cellars – you never knew what might be lurking in them. Ooh, look it was a downstairs—

Aargh!

A flurry of brown feathers and a volley of indignant squawks greeted her, as another one of those blasted chickens shot between her legs.

Dulcie recoiled in alarm, her heart hammering as she choked back a scream, and she put her hand to her chest, willing herself to calm down.

It was only a chicken. Surely she could handle this?

But it had horrid scaley legs like a reptile, and long talons at the end of its toes. And it was **looking** at her. A beady eye watched her warily, as both human and bird froze.

 'Shoo?' Dulcie's voice was hesitant, more of a timid request than a forthright command.

The chicken uttered a low clucking sound and bobbed its head in response.

How had it got in, anyway? And what was it doing in the bathroom? Shower room, she amended, as she took her eyes off the horrid creature to glance around the room. Oh, god, she hoped it wasn't the only bathroom. The thought of having to traipse downstairs in the middle of the night if she needed a wee, filled her with dread. Maybe that was what the bucket was for, she suddenly thought, horrified.

The chicken chucked again, although the noise was less of a cluck and more of a throaty warble.

She would worry about bathrooms later: she had a chicken to deal with first.

Slowly, so as not to alarm it and run the risk of it attacking her, Dulcie sidled towards the back door. A key was in the lock, so she turned it, grateful when she heard a snick as the mechanism engaged, and she eased the door open, then retreated to a safe distance.

The chicken stared at her, and she stared back at the chicken. For a moment Dulcie thought it was going to refuse to leave, but then its head shot forward, seeming to pull the rest of its feathery body with it as it took a step towards the door.

As soon as it was safely outside, Dulcie slammed the door shut, then turned her attention to the open window in the shower room, and closed that firmly, too.

Look at the mess the creature had made, she thought, eying a snowstorm of shredded white paper which was all that was left of a loo roll, except for the empty cardboard tube which still hung on the holder. Some of the decimated tissue paper had been scuffed into a pile, and for one awful moment Dulcie feared that the chicken had done a poo on it.

Wrinkling her nose in disgust, she peered at the mess and wondered where in the numerous boxes in the car she would find some rubber gloves, when she realised that the poo was, in fact, an egg. A brown egg which was still warm, she discovered when she picked it up, and she smiled. Her very first egg.

It was as though the chicken had left her a welcome-to-your-new-home present, and her heart thawed a little towards it.

Gingerly she carried the egg into the kitchen and left it in the sink whilst she explored the rest of the house.

The remainder of the downstairs consisted of a nice-sized living room to the other side of the hall, and even before Dulcie had ventured up the stairs to the first floor, she was imagining how it would look if the hideous carpet was replaced with floorboards or quarry tiles. She would keep it as a family room, she decided. It was large enough for a couple of big squashy sofas, or an L-shaped one might be a good idea, considering how big her family was and that they would no doubt all want to come for a visit at exactly the same time.

The smaller sitting room, the one off the kitchen, could be turned into a dining room, although the kitchen itself was roomy enough for a table, and one was already in there. The last person to have lived in this house was an older gent, and the solicitor had informed her that much of the furniture had been left in situ and was now hers, so she decided that she would drag the table into the dining room.

Dulcie was grateful for some of the furniture because furnishing a house this size was beyond her immediate means, yet she ungratefully wished that the heavy dark-wood wardrobes and chests of drawers which were in all five of the bedrooms, were a bit more stylish. Still, they would do for now, although she had every intention of making the purchase of a new mattress to go on the brass bedstead in the master bedroom her number one priority. She would have to sleep on the old one tonight though, and she prayed that the former owner hadn't breathed his last on it.

No wonder Walter York hadn't removed any of the furniture but had left it for the new owner – aka Dulcie – to dispose of. He probably hadn't wanted the hassle. So now it had become her hassle instead.

He might have warned her that the interior of the house needed a complete overhaul, though. He also could have informed her that there was a chicken in her downstairs loo. But he hadn't said a word, and she wondered what else Walter York hadn't told her.

She soon found out when she tried to call her mum to let her know that she had arrived safely, only to discover that there was no phone signal. None whatsoever.

Damn Walter York.

Otto's dad pounced on him as soon as Otto stepped inside the door of the former stockman's cottage that was now his father's (and his) new home. Thank goodness Otto had made sure that the cottage and a small paddock hadn't been part of the deal when he had raffled off the farm.

The farm had actually belonged to his father, Walter, and Otto had had a devil of a job trying to convince him that it had to be sold – because how else would the farm's horrendous debts be paid off? Besides, his dad was no longer in any fit state to work the land and run the farm. And even if he had been fit and healthy enough, Walter was the other side of seventy, so how much longer could he have continued?

'Well, what's she like?' his dad demanded.

It was only April, so the weather wasn't the best, and in the short amount of time between driving down the lane from the farm and arriving at Muddypuddle Lane Cottage the drizzle had turned to rain. His dad was sitting in front of a roaring fire, with a blanket tucked around his legs. He looked frail and unwell, and Otto's stomach turned over. His dad was improving slowly, but he had a long way to go, and Otto wasn't sure he was out of the woods yet.

'Young, clueless,' Otto replied, running his hands through his hair to shake off the droplets of rainwater. A dog's nose booped him on the leg, and he bent to pat her. She was a black and white Border collie by the name of Peg, and his dad had owned her since she was a pup. It would have devastated him to be parted from her. He would have also been upset to be parted from Flossie, the sheep he had hand-reared last year. Walter had formed an unusual attachment to the lamb, so much so that he had visibly shrunk when Otto had informed him that he had planned on selling her along with the rest of the flock.

Otto had relented and Flossie now lived in the small paddock to the side of the cottage; although she did have a tendency to prefer being inside the cottage itself and could often be found lying on the rug next to his dad's chair in the sitting room and happily chewing the cud, much to Otto's consternation. It was bad enough having the dog wandering in and out of the house, and Puss too, when the cat deigned to pay them a visit. A sheep was the last straw.

'How young? She's not on her own, is she?' Walter sat forward, concern on his craggy face.

'She appears to be.'

His dad began to fret. 'She's not going to be able to manage that place on her own. You're going to have to help her. I would do it myself, but...' He ground to a halt, not needing to say anything further. They both knew that Walter not being able to do it himself was the reason why he had to get rid of the farm in the first place.

'No chance,' Otto spluttered. He'd be damned if he was going to go running up the lane every time Dulcie Fairfax flipped her lid at the sight of a hen. If she couldn't cope on her own, she should have thought about that before she bought a lottery ticket.

He caught his dad's expression as he went to make a cup of tea, and Walter's grumbling followed him out to the kitchen.

Otto knew that letting the farm go had been hard on the old man, but what else could he have done? By the time Otto realised that his dad was struggling and discovered that he had run up huge debts, including getting a mortgage on the farm, it had been almost too late to pull back from the brink of bankruptcy. If that had happened his father would have lost everything, including the cottage they now lived in. Walter would probably have ended up in a rented house where he wouldn't have been able to take either of his animals. It would have destroyed him.

Otto had returned to the farm to try to save it, but after having it valued and realising that even if the property achieved its full asking price, it wouldn't be enough to pay off all his dad's creditors, Otto had almost lost hope. Until, that is, he had seen an advert on tv.

It was for a prize draw to win a rather expensive house.

With little real hope, he had begun to look into how a prize draw such as that worked, and he had been amazed to discover that it might be a way out of their situation.

And so, after a great deal of research and a lot of soul-searching, Otto had eventually offered the farm up as a prize draw, with the proceeds (after all the debts on the farm had been paid) going to charity.

He hadn't honestly expected much interest.

But there had been loads, and the lucky winner was now settling into the house that had been in his family for generations, and where he had grown up.

To say he felt resentful was an understatement, but Otto just had to suck it up and get on with it. Today was the start of a new normal for him and his dad. With the farm no longer their responsibility and the transfer complete, Otto could try to look to the future, starting with getting a job. He knew it might be quite some time until he returned to London and the restaurant scene – his dad needed him here – but he couldn't not work. For a start, he needed the income, and for another, he had to keep busy. The thought of not working in a commercial kitchen and not being able to conjure up mouth-watering dishes made his heart ache. He was a chef and a damned good one, and he didn't know how to do anything else.

But the issue was, cheffing usually involved unreasonable hours, and long ones too. And the only eateries in Picklewick were The Black Horse and a couple of cafes, which meant he would have to look further afield for a job as a chef. But if that was the case, once he factored in the commuting time, just how much would he be able to care for his dad if he was out of the house for hours on end?

There was one small ray of sunshine in the cloudy sky which was Otto's life right now, and that was his dad's health. His father might hate that the farm had gone, but even in the short amount of time since he had moved into Muddypuddle Cottage, Otto could already see an improvement. His father seemed brighter, more with it, and not so frail or forgetful.

Maybe it was the stress and worry that had been making him ill, and if that was the case then Otto might be able to think about going back to proper cheffing work in the not-to-distant future. However, it would be a while yet, so he'd better ask around and see if he could find something local to tide him over.

There was nothing else for it: Dulcie would have to get in her car and drive to somewhere that **did** have a signal. Apart from venturing outside or going into the attic (she had eyed the hatch set into the ceiling at the top of the stairs with horror) she had tried everything without any luck, to get a signal.

She had wandered into every room in the house, peering intently at her phone and praying to see some bars. Just one would do – she wasn't greedy – but even after standing on the beds, waving her arm out of all the windows, and going as far as to clamber onto the toilet seat and stretch the phone above her head, she still couldn't raise a peep out of it.

Reluctantly, and keeping her eyes peeled for marauding chickens, Dulcie shot across the farmyard and dived into her car, wishing she had worn her raincoat – although how much use it would be in this deluge was debatable.

With great care, she steered the Fiat out of the yard, her attention glued on the dirt track as she tried in vain to remember where the most lethal potholes were. The problem was that they had filled up with rainwater, so it was difficult to tell a deep hole from a shallow puddle, and she inched down the lane with a great deal of caution, until she reached the turn-off to the stables. Coming to a standstill, she risked a glance at her phone and her heart leapt when she saw the screen.

Finally, she had a signal!

'Mum? It's me, Dulcie!' she cried, as soon as her mum answered.

'Oh, hi love, can I call you back, I'm just in the middle of—'

'No, you can't!' Dulcie shouted. No way was she going to sit in the car for goodness knows how long and wait for her mum to phone her back. 'It's now or never,' she said.

'Calm down, Drama Queen. I was only going to—'

'Mum, I'm sitting in my car in the pouring rain. I need to speak to you **now!**'

'Are you lost? Have you broken down?'

'No. I found the farm okay, but there's no phone signal.'

'Is that all? I thought something major had happened.' Her mum chuckled and added, 'Although, I suppose the farm not having a signal **is** the end of the world for you.'

Dulcie rolled her eyes. Her mum was just as attached to her own mobile. It was the easiest way to keep in touch with all four of her kids.

'Anyway, I thought I'd let you know that I've arrived safe and sound,' Dulcie said, huffily. 'I'll leave you to get on with what you were doing.'

'It can wait. Now that you're on the line you might as well tell me what the farm is like. And how was your journey? Have you eaten?'

Ah, this was more like it, Dulcie thought, wondering where to begin. She'd start with the easiest questions first. 'The journey was fine, and I stopped off for a sandwich and a coffee on the way. As for the farm...' She was desperate to share her disappointment with her mum, as well as her concern that she might have bitten off more than she could chew, but she didn't want to worry her. Anyway, she had only been here an hour, which was hardly long enough to get a proper feel for the place. And the reality was never going to live up to her expectations – Dulcie knew she shouldn't have spent so much time on the internet, gazing at photos of gorgeous barn conversions and baby ducklings...

Instead, she said, 'It's raining at the moment and there's a lot of mist, so I haven't had a chance to look around yet, but it seems very... **farmy**. There are loads of fields and from where I'm sitting I can see horses.'

'I thought you told me that there wouldn't be any animals?'

'I expect they belong to the stables. Remember me telling you that there was a stables nearby? I showed you on Google Earth? I've had to drive as far as that to get a signal.'

'Have you seen the house yet?'

'I have.' Dulcie nodded, even though her mum couldn't see her.

'Well?'

'It's rustic...' she began, wanting to pick her words carefully.

'Oh, I'm so pleased! That's what you were hoping for,' her mum said.

It was, but Dulcie hadn't anticipated this degree of rusticness – if there was such a word.

'You'll have to send us some pictures, and as soon as you've unpacked I expect an invite,' her mum declared.

Yeah, that was what Dulcie had been afraid of. She had gone from demanding that her family come visit her as soon as was humanly possible, to wondering how long she could hold them off. She should never have crowed about winning the farm, but she hadn't been able to stop herself. If only she had held back a little, her mother, sisters and brother wouldn't be under the impression that the farm was the best thing since sliced bread. She should have waited until she'd seen it first. Maybe the place would look better with a coat of paint, and some pretty cushions.

'It's really olde-worlde,' she said, 'with beams in all the rooms, a wonderful flagstone floor in the dining room and a log burner, and an open fireplace in the sitting room. It's even got a pantry, and a shower room downstairs.'

She didn't tell her that the beams were probably dust-magnets, that there were hideous carpets in most of the rooms and that she had found a chicken in the loo.

Dulcie continued, 'The previous owner has left most of the furniture, and I'm sure one or two pieces are quite old. They might even be antiques.'

She failed to mention that old was a euphemism for decrepit. And neither did she say that she had met the former owner and his attitude had left a lot to be desired.

'It sounds lovely,' her mum said, dreamily. 'I wish you'd have let me or Maisie come with you to help you move in. She's at a loose end today.'

'Loose end?' Dulcie narrowed her eyes. 'Don't tell me she's lost yet another job?'

Her mum hesitated. 'She didn't lose it. She walked out.'

'When was this?'

'Last night. Shifts don't agree with her.'

Dulcie thought that it wasn't shift work that didn't agree with her younger sister – it was work itself. In the five years since

Maisie had left college, she had flitted from job to job and from boyfriend to boyfriend. She seemed unable to stick to anything, or anyone.

Their mother claimed that Maisie just hadn't found her place in the world yet.

Dulcie reckoned that Maisie never would. As the youngest of the family, her sister had been indulged and babied. She was still being indulged and babied at twenty-four. When Dulcie was Maisie's age, she had a flat of her own (albeit rented) and had held down a decent job for a couple of years.

'Er, that's okay. Mum,' she said. She could do without Maisie's brand of helping – which consisted of getting in the way, whilst not doing a lot. Her sister was an expert at it.

Anyway, Dulcie had wanted her first view of the farm to be when she was alone, undiluted by the opinions of her mum or her siblings. And now, she was glad that she hadn't brought any of them with her.

She chatted with her mum for a while longer, and after saying goodbye she made a few calls to some broadband providers, and to British Telecom to ask how she could get the landline working. It was imperative that she had access to the internet, because her job depended on it.

There was one advantage to living in the middle of nowhere she decided, brightening up when she was told that she would be online by the end of the week, and that was there should be little risk of interruption, so she could work in peace.

Her job as a customer services advisor for an energy provider, meant that she often dealt with things of a sensitive nature, and the last thing customers wanted to hear was the sound of a police siren in the road outside, or loud music blaring from the inconsiderate moron who had lived in the flat above hers. And neither did they want to hear next door's toddler having a meltdown, or a car alarm going off in the street below her window.

Look on the positive side, she told herself: she owned the farm outright, and although it mightn't be how she'd imagined it, it was nevertheless hers.

In fact, she was looking forward to the peace and quiet.

CHAPTER THREE

For once in her life, Dulcie was glad to roll out of bed. She'd had one of the worst night's sleep ever, and she would have got up earlier but she wanted to wait until it was light so she didn't feel as though she was getting up in the middle of the night.

She had gotten up a couple of times, though. Fear had driven her from her bed to stand barefoot by the closed bedroom door, as she strained to work out what was making the noises and where they were coming from. Scratching, scrabbling, the patter of scurrying feet and squeaking, and once or twice an unearthly shriek had her quaking in terror and had sent her dashing back to the safety of the bed, where she'd pulled the duvet over her head, curled into a ball and clamped her hands to her ears.

Finally, at some point, she had drifted off, but her sleep had been fitful and uneasy, and she was relieved when the sun rose and she could get up.

Her bedroom didn't look much better today, she thought, as she shoved her feet into her slippers. She had spent the rest of yesterday unloading the car, cleaning, and trying to settle in, and she was already sick of scrubbing. But much of what she had thought was dirt, was just age. Torn lino, cracked tiles, peeling wallpaper. Her first impression had been right – the place needed gutting. But without having the financial means to take the farmhouse back to bare stone and start again, she was stuck with making the best of what she had.

One thing she could be thankful for, was that the house had been rewired a few years ago, so that was one less expense to worry about, although Walter York hadn't stretched to putting in a new boiler or radiators. These were so old, they were probably back in fashion once more as retro items.

That was a thought...assuming they still conducted heat and didn't leak, perhaps she could strip them and repaint them?

Thankfully the boiler worked, as she had discovered yesterday when she had run the tap and hot water had flowed from it. She didn't know what she would have done if it hadn't, but she made a note to herself to get someone out to check it anyway.

Suddenly her knees gave way and she plopped onto the mattress.

Was this going to be too much for her to handle? She knew she was vacillating between wanting to make a go of it one minute, and wanting to throw in the towel the next, but she'd never had to face anything like this before.

Should she pack up and go home? She might have been tempted if she had somewhere to go back to, but she had given up the lease on her flat and her flatmate had moved out to live with her girlfriend. The only other option was to move back in with her mother, but although she loved her mum to bits, Dulcie would prefer to dig her own eyeballs out with a blunt spoon than to live with her.

Her older sister, Nikki, didn't have a spare room, Maisie still lived at home, and Jay, their brother, was in Asia somewhere, installing acoustic sensors in treetops (something to do with conservation), so none of her siblings was an option either.

With a sigh, Dulcie trotted downstairs, still in her jammies. It was a cow onesie actually, bought in a fit of excitement when she'd learned that she had won the farm, and it was lovely and snuggly.

Despondently thinking that she had made her bed and so would have to lie in it, she suddenly noticed the sun beaming through the sitting room window and saw the view that lay beyond the glass, and her heart lifted. The scenery was magnificent – lush green fields stretching down the hillside, and a view across the valley. And when she went into the kitchen to make coffee, she saw that the view from there was just as lovely. The garden might be overgrown but it was dotted with wildflowers and beyond it must be the orchard. She wondered where the stream was, and she vowed to go exploring later. First, though, she needed some breakfast.

Thankful that she'd had the foresight to bring supplies such as bread, butter, milk and coffee with her (she had cooked herself an omelette last night, although she hadn't plucked up the courage to use the egg that the chicken had left for her), Dulcie set about making some toast.

She had just sat down to eat it, her gaze roaming around the kitchen and thinking that the room didn't look as gloomy this morning as it had yesterday, when she almost leapt out of her chair as the back door banged open and the figure of a man barged through it.

Dulcie let out a scream and dropped her toast, butter-side down, then let out another yell as a fluttery brown ball of feathers darted between the man's legs and lunged at it.

In a mad scramble, she climbed onto the chair she had been sitting on and brandished a teaspoon. She had no idea what use it would be, but it had been the nearest implement to hand and it was better than nothing. And neither did she know who to use it on first, the chicken or Walter York.

'Get that thing away from me,' she screeched, balancing on one leg to try to give the chicken less of a target should it choose to attack.

The hen ignored her. It was too busy pecking at the toast, and with every stab of its beak, Dulcie's breakfast was flung into the air, the chicken darting after it.

'That "thing" is your responsibility,' Walter yelled at her, and Dulcie blinked at him, the wind momentarily taken out of her sails.

'What?' she asked, then rallied before he could say another word. 'How dare you come barging in here as though you own the place. May I remind you that you don't!' Fury was beginning to replace her initial fear, and she let him have it with both barrels. 'Get out **now!** Or I'll call the police,' she added, then winced as she remembered that she couldn't get a mobile signal and the landline wasn't in service either.

'*I* should be the one calling the police,' he shot back. 'Or the RSPCA. You're not fit to look after a woodlouse, let alone a chicken.'

'I didn't realise they needed looking after,' Dulcie retorted crossly, getting down from her perch as that insufferable man ushered the chicken out of her kitchen. It had left several little feathers behind, as well as a blob of something disgusting on the flagstones. 'I thought they, you know, scratched around and found their own food,' she added. 'What do they eat, anyway?' She eyed the blob with distaste.

'Spiders, caterpillars, other insects, poultry feed, but that's not what I'm talking about. You left them out last night,' he accused.

'What else was I supposed to do with them? Invite them to share my bed? It was bad enough finding one in the downstairs loo.'

'You're supposed to lock them in their coop.'

'Why? Frankly, I don't care if they run away.'

'I wouldn't blame them if they did. But they're more likely to be eaten.'

'You wouldn't!'

'Not *me*, you idiot – although I've got nothing against a nice plump bird. I was referring to a fox.'

The way he looked her up and down made her think that he was calling her a plump bird, but then she realised what he'd said.

'A fox?' she repeated.

'Yeah, you know...looks a bit like a dog, russet coloured, bushy tail? Gobbles up chickens for supper?'

'Are they alright?'

'They are. No thanks to you.'

'I didn't know, did I? You should have told me. Where is the coop anyway?' She took a wet wipe out of the cupboard under the sink and cleared away the offending blob.

'If you'd like to get dressed, I'll show you.'

Dulcie became aware that she was still in her night things, and she suddenly felt incredibly self-conscious. She might think her cow onesie was cute, but from the sneering expression on his face, Walter didn't think so.

'Look, Walter,' she began, her dander rising again. If he hadn't barged into her house without knocking, then he wouldn't have had his delicate senses assaulted by the sight of her in her cow onesie.

'Walter?' He looked over his shoulder. 'Where?'

'What?'

'My dad.'

'Your dad?'

'What about him?' he asked.

'What?' Dulcie repeated, wondering what he was talking about.

'You just mentioned his name'

'I didn't.'

'You did!'

She growled in exasperation. 'I said no such thing. What I was going to say before I was so rudely interrupted, was that you had no right to enter my house. I demand you give me the key.' She held out her hand.

'I don't have a key.'

'How did you get in, then?' she cried triumphantly.

'The door wasn't locked.'

Dulcie blinked. 'It wasn't?'

He shook his head. 'No.'

Oh god, she'd forgotten to lock the back door after she'd let the chicken out yesterday. She had been upstairs **all night** with an unlocked door! Anything could have happened.

'Walter, I—' she began, but he rudely interrupted her for a second time. The man was insufferable. Grr.

'Why do you keep saying my dad's—' he began, then his frown cleared. 'Ah, now I get it. You think **I'm** Walter.' He poked himself in the chest.

Dulcie wanted to poke him in the eye. 'Aren't you?'

'I'm Otto. Walter is my father.'

Dulcie blinked again. 'Your **father?** But it was you who handed me the keys.'

'I did.'

'I see.' But Dulcie didn't see at all. If Walter was Otto's father, why had Otto allowed him to live in such a pigsty when he himself was clearly well off? It was a disgrace.

Otto pulled a face. 'Well? Are you going to get dressed, or are you coming outside in your...whatever it is you're wearing. I haven't got all day.'

It took her a second to remember what they had been talking about. 'I'm sure I can find the chicken coop by myself, thank you,' she said, haughtily. 'And I'd appreciate it if you didn't barge into my house like you still own it. You don't.'

His eyebrows shot up. She had the feeling he wasn't used to people standing up to him or answering him back. Maybe he had expected her to doff her cap or curtsey, and apologise profusely. She had a mind to tell him it was his father's fault that the chickens nearly ended up as fox food, because the contract quite clearly stated that the transaction didn't involve livestock. She might be mistaken, but surely chickens counted as livestock?

However, the birds were on her property and appeared to be her responsibility now, and although they gave her the heebie-jeebies, she didn't want to see any of them gobbled up by a hungry fox.

Otto glared at her sullenly for a moment and Dulcie glared back, determined not to be intimidated by him. The standoff ended when he shook his head, turned smartly on his heel and marched out.

To her intense irritation, he had left the door open and she hurried to close it, worried that the chicken might decide to return. It clearly liked it in the house, and she wondered whether it had been given free rein to come and go as it pleased. The thought made her shudder.

Debating whether to make herself any more toast, she realised she had lost her appetite, so she made her way upstairs to get dressed.

She had managed to unpack all her clothes yesterday, but on opening her wardrobe in the cold light of day, she realised she was woefully unprepared for this new life of hers. Cute playsuits, smart blazers and frilly blouses weren't suitable clothing for rounding chickens up, or for traipsing about muddy farmyards. She did have some loungey-type leggings and tee shirts though, which would have to do for the time being. She'd shove a fleece over the top and wear her oldest pair of boots or trainers, but what she could really do with was a pair of wellies.

Perhaps she would take a trip into the village later for some supplies, and see if any of the shops stocked Wellington boots. She wondered if Cath Kidston did wellies – she quite fancied something pretty and floral. But then again, even if she found somewhere in Picklewick that stocked that particular brand, she probably wouldn't be able to afford it. Her mum had always accused her of having champagne tastes on beer money, and she was right.

Dulcie couldn't help it if she liked nice things...

Grimacing, she dragged one of her least favourite tee shirts over her head and pulled a pair of joggers out of a drawer, then went outside to find the chicken coop.

The morning light brought her to a halt before she had taken more than a couple of steps and she gazed around in wonder. Everything was so clean and clear, and she took a deep breath of fresh air, inhaling the scent of flowers and growing things. She could also smell a faint animal aroma, and she narrowed her eyes at the horses grazing in the fields below, guessing that it was a smell she would have to get used to if she intended to stay.

The jury was still out on that one, but she had a sneaking suspicion that she was going to give it a go, surmising that she might regret it if she didn't.

Stepping gingerly because there was still a considerable amount of mud around, as well as puddles from yesterday's rain and a coating of green moss in places, Dulcie wandered around the farmyard, peering into barns and peeping around corners, trying to get her bearings.

It seemed that there was one large barn which had empty pens in it and a strong smell of something nasty, plus another one which was open-sided and contained a few pieces of rusting metal and something that looked as though it might have been a tractor in another life. Then there was a stone building that had lots of different rooms, and held stuff she didn't want to examine too closely.

She did find a big sack of something called Layers Pellets, which had a picture of a chicken and an egg on the front, so she hoped she had found the bird food. She also found several stacked bales of straw and one of the chickens, which was perched on top of a bale. It was in a stand-off with a substantial ginger cat, the same one that had been in the photograph, and which was now sitting on the ground below the bale, its tail curled around its feet and studying the chicken intently.

It seemed that neither animal was backing down, and she hoped there wouldn't be a scuffle. The cat looked like it meant business, but so did the chicken. It was looking at her out of one beady eye, its beak open, and it made a burbling noise.

The cat's response was to swish its tail and ignore Dulcie, which was fine by her because she preferred dogs anyway.

Then it suddenly occurred to her that she might be responsible for *this* animal's welfare also, and she wondered whether it was eyeing the chicken as a potential breakfast item because she had failed to feed it, and her heart sank.

At least she had discovered the chicken pellets, so she could feed one of her charges. The cat would have to wait until she went into the village later.

Ripping open the bag, she was just wondering what she should use to put the pellets in, when three things happened at once. None of them good.

The chicken uttered an excited squawk and launched itself at her head.

The cat launched itself at the chicken, ending up with its claws in her fleece and its whiskery catface inches from hers, making Dulcie stagger back, and in doing so she upended the sack and pellets scattered everywhere.

Then she was butted in the backside by a sheep.

Not that she realised it was a sheep at first because all she was aware of was a thump on the behind, which sent her toppling forwards. But when she regained her balance, a huge white woolly thing with a black nose and black eyes was lining up to charge at her.

Dulcie let out a bloodcurdling scream that shocked the sheep long enough for her to get a head start on it, as she sprinted for the farmhouse door.

She didn't think she imagined its hot breath on her legs as she dashed across the yard, and she certainly didn't imagine the excited bleats it made as it almost caught her.

Reaching the door, she careened through it, and for an awful second she thought the sheep was going to come right in after her, but she managed to slam it shut on the creature's rabid nose.

Panting, her heart thumping and her knees shaking, Dulcie leant against the door and promptly burst into tears.

CHAPTER FOUR

Otto stormed down the hill in much the same way as he had stormed up it, minus a chicken under his arm.

He had discovered the poor thing early this morning, when he had let Peg out for a wee. It had been hiding in the hedge, looking disorientated and rather sorry for itself, and realising that it was one of his dad's hens, Otto guessed that Dulcie hadn't shut them in for the night.

Furious at her lack of regard for the creatures in her care, he had gathered up the hen and marched up the lane. Spying another bird dart around the side of the farmhouse, looking equally as bedraggled as the one under his arm, he had chased after it, but it had disappeared. At that point, he had found himself standing directly outside the backdoor. Totally irate by now, he had raised his fist to give the door a damned good hammering, but to his shock it had flown open under the force of his powerful knock.

Otto had stumbled inside, nearly falling flat on his face, and had dropped the chicken as he tried to remain upright. Then all hell had broken loose.

He knew it must have been a shock to have him barge into the kitchen, but Dulcie needn't have acted like he was about to attack her. And what on earth had she been thinking, hopping onto a chair and waving a spoon around? Was she going to **spoon** him to death?

Without warning, an image of the two of them in bed, his arms around her as she spooned into him had flashed across his inner eye, and he had nearly turned tail and scarpered. If it hadn't been for the hen throwing a piece of toast in the air as it tried to peck off a morsel, and reminding him of the reason for his impromptu visit, Otto might have done just that.

Instead, he had yelled at her, and she had screeched back at him, and then an odd conversation had ensued where she had thought he was his father and he had thought that she had lost the plot.

And what the hell had she been **wearing?** He knew enough about female nightwear to know that it was a onesie, but it had looked suspiciously like she was in a fancy-dress cow costume.

She had looked darned cute in it, though.

His stomping slowed as he neared the cottage and his ire began to dissipate as he was forced to acknowledge that the issue with the hens last night wasn't necessarily Dulcie's fault.

It was his.

The responsibility for re-homing the livestock had been down to him. Not his dad. He had overlooked the chickens, too wrapped up in disposing of the larger critters on the farm. They had gone to market in batches, ewes with their lambs, and he had sold all of them apart from Flossie. The process had taken more time and effort than he had anticipated, and he hadn't given finding new homes for the three hens a second thought. Apart from collecting a couple of eggs everyday and remembering to secure them in their coop at night and letting them out the following morning, they hadn't crossed his mind.

Until today.

Oh, shit, now he was starting to feel guilty about having a go at her, and shame blossomed in his chest. He shouldn't have expected a city girl like her (and she clearly *was* a city girl) to know how to care for hens. Especially since she had been informed that no animals remained on the farm. When he had seen her reaction to the chicken, he should have advised her that they would need caring for. But he had been so overwhelmed with sadness, regret and shame because he hadn't realised just how bad things had got, that—

Oh, who was he kidding? Yes, he had felt all of those things, as well as disbelief that he was about to hand over the keys to his family farm to a complete stranger, who didn't know the first thing about farming. But he had also felt something else, something which had taken him by complete surprise – and that was attraction. Attraction that he still felt and which, if anything, had grown since he had first set eyes on Dulcie yesterday.

There was nothing else for it. In order to assuage his guilt, he would have to apologise. So he may as well do it now, and get it over with. Besides, he wouldn't mind another look at her in that cute onesie...

Turning smartly on his heel, Otto headed back up the hill.

Luckily it wasn't far to walk from the cottage to the farmhouse.

Initially, he had worried that the lack of distance between the two properties would be a major issue for his dad when he had eventually managed to convince his father that the only way out of the financial mess Walter had found himself in was to get rid of everything except the cottage and the small parcel of land it stood on. He had moved into the cottage itself, and Otto had been concerned that being so near to the farm, yet no longer owning it, might prove to be the final straw for his father.

Walter had indeed found it difficult – the farm was all he knew, and the only place he had ever lived – but he seemed to be coping, and Otto was quietly hopeful that his dad would settle into a new routine and a new way of living.

Otto hoped the same applied to him, and that he, himself, would settle into a new routine: when he actually discovered what that new routine might be. It would begin if (*when*) he found a job, and he vowed to start looking in earnest later today.

He heard a cacophony of squawks coming from the barn as he rounded the corner into the yard, his sturdy boots splashing through the last of yesterday's puddles, and wondered what could be causing the racket.

When he took a look, he discovered that Puss, the unimaginatively named ginger tomcat who had flatly refused to go live in the cottage and insisted on taking up residence in one of the barns instead, was teasing the hens. A pile of poultry feed was spilling out of an upturned sack and the birds were squabbling amongst themselves as they tried to gobble up as many pellets as was chickenly possible.

Scattering the agitated hens, Otto waded through them and reached for the sack, hefted it into his arms and took it to one of the metal bins next to the stacked bales of hay, where he lifted the lid and dropped it in.

The hens looked on in dismay.

Otto frowned. 'You've got enough to be going on with,' he told them, jerking his chin at the ground where a substantial number of pellets still lay. 'You lot won't need feeding for a week. I'd better see some decent eggs from you after all this food,' he warned, before remembering that whatever they laid would now belong to Dulcie.

He wondered whether she had found the coop yet, or whether she had even bothered to look.

'Go do something useful and catch a mouse or two,' he told the cat, who was glaring at him. The animal was in a sphinx position with his tail curled around his paws, and the tip of it twitched in irritation.

There was no way Puss could be described as a lap-cat. He was the least friendly feline Otto had ever known, and the animal was as hard as nails to boot. Puss would stand his ground against a charging bull, and Otto wouldn't bet on the bull's chances of getting away unscathed.

Leaving Puss where he was, Otto headed towards the front of the house, mindful that he should knock properly this time. But as he drew nearer, he realised he could hear the insistent bleating of a sheep coming from around the back, and he guessed Flossie must have escaped again.

'Flossie,' he called, knowing that the ewe would recognise her name. Whether she would respond to it was a different matter entirely. It hadn't yet sunk into her woolly head that Walter, who had bottle-fed her from birth, no longer resided in the farmhouse, and Otto knew she was probably demanding her breakfast. For Flossie, the usual sheep's fare of grass wasn't good enough. Despite being a year old and fully weaned, she wanted milk and was quite vociferous in making her wishes known.

Ah, there she was, standing on the step, bleating insistently and giving the door an occasional cheeky bump with her head. He was about to catch hold of her woolly shoulder and drag her away, when he paused.

Was that a shriek he could hear?

The ewe bleated again and butted the door, which rattled in its frame, and immediately another shriek followed, accompanied by Dulcie's voice yelling, 'Go away, please go away!'

'Dulcie?' he called, reaching the step. 'Are you okay?'

'Of course I'm not okay. What a stupid question! That sheep tried to kill me. Take it away!'

Otto pressed his lips together to stop himself from laughing when he saw the pale disc of her face peering through the window of the utility room.

'She just wants a bottle. But don't give her one,' he added hastily.

'I've no intention of giving her anything,' Dulcie called back. 'Am I right in thinking this thing belongs to you?'

'To my dad, yes.'

'Then if anything happens to me, I'll hold you responsible.'

'Nothing is going to happen to you,' he assured her, but at that precise moment Flossie decided to give the door an extra hard bang, and it rattled alarmingly in its frame.

Dulcie screeched and clapped her hands to her cheeks. 'Get it away from me!' she shouted.

Gosh, she was really scared, he realised, and wasn't just being a drama queen. 'Wait there,' he instructed, but as he began to walk away he heard her cry, 'Don't leave me. It might get in.'

'It won't,' he called over his shoulder. 'I'm just going to fetch a rope.'

Years ago, his dad used to show sheep, and had won a few rosettes in his time too, so there were still a couple of halters on the premises and he soon found one, plus a lead rope to clip onto it, and hurried back to the house.

Expertly, he slipped the halter onto Flossie's head, then led her away to tie her to one of the posts next to the gate to the veggie patch.

'See, she's tame,' he said. 'You can come out now.'

'I don't think so,' Dulcie retorted, her nose squashed against the glass. 'Not until you get it off my property.'

Otto held up his hands in mock surrender. 'Okay, there's no need to get upset. She's perfectly harmless.'

'In case you hadn't noticed, I am **already** upset. The horrid thing attacked me.'

'She didn't,' Otto insisted.

'How do you know? You weren't here.'

No, but he wished he had been. He had a feeling it would have been funny.

His amusement must have shown on his face, because Dulcie slapped a hand to the glass.

'Don't you dare laugh!' she cried. 'If I see that animal again, I'm going to phone the police or the RSPCA.'

Otto's amusement quickly faded as she threw his own words back in his face.

How dare she! She didn't know the first thing about caring for animals, yet she was threatening to report **him** to the authorities.

'Fine,' he said, shortly. 'I'll make sure that the new owner of Lilac Tree **Farm**—' he emphasised the last word with drawling sarcasm '—isn't bothered by a farm animal ever again. Would you like me to remove the chickens whilst I'm at it? How about the cat? Although you might like him to stay to keep the mice down. I'm afraid I can't do anything about those because they're not classed as livestock. Neither are the birds in the trees, or the insects in the garden.' He knew he was ranting, but that woman was bringing out the worst in him.

He threw his hands in the air in disgust and marched over to Flossie.

'Wait!' she shouted. 'What do you mean, **mice?** There aren't any mice.' A pause. 'Are there?'

'I'll think you'll find that there are,' he said, grimly pleased that he had managed to put a dent in her self-righteous anger.

'Like, in the fields?' she asked.

'Like, in the house,' he replied. 'You can hear them in the walls.'

Her horrified expression was to remain with him for the rest of the day.

But it was only when he was freeing Flossie from her halter and setting her loose in the paddock, did he realise that he hadn't apologised, and he was glad that he hadn't. Dulcie didn't deserve his apology. What she deserved was his contempt, and she had that in spades.

Seriously, being without a phone signal was the pits, Dulcie concluded, as she dug into an early lunch in The Black Horse, her phone propped up in front of her.

After the trauma of sheepgate, Dulcie had hurried upstairs to change into something more respectable, then had fled to Picklewick, bouncing her little car over the potholes without a second thought to any damage to its suspension. She had to get away from the farm right this minute, and Picklewick was the nearest thing to civilisation.

She had parked in the high street and then remained inside the vehicle for a few minutes, drinking in the welcome sight of people going about their normal everyday activities. She would bet her last pound that none of **them** had been attacked by a sheep this morning. She was still shaking from the experience, despite Otto putting a lead on it like it was a dog, to show her how tame it was.

After a quick coffee in one of the cafes to steady her nerves, she had explored the village.

Her delight had been unfeigned. Picklewick was quaint and pretty, and she was relieved to find that her first impression yesterday hadn't been wrong. Was it only **yesterday** that she had driven along this very same street, full of dreams and unbridled excitement? It might only be twenty-four hours, but to her it felt like a lifetime.

Telling herself that things could only get better, she purchased some paint, a wallpaper scraper, brushes and anything else in the decorating department of the small hardware store that she thought she might need, then went in search of a pair of wellies and a more practical coat.

She'd found both in a shop that seemed to cater to outdoorsy farming folk, and although the Wellington boots were a dismayingly drab shade of green (not a

Cath Kidston print in sight) they would do the trick.

Shopping done, she had decided to grab a bite to eat before she returned to the farm. After having her breakfast so rudely interrupted, Dulcie was starving. She didn't fancy cooking when she got back (did she *ever* fancy cooking? – she was the most reluctant and uninspiring cook she knew), and she suspected that she would want to get stuck into the decorating and not want the faff of preparing a meal, even if it was only a sandwich. If she ate something substantial now, it would set her up for the rest of the day, which was why she was currently sitting at a corner table in the pub, wielding a fork in one hand and blissfully scrolling the internet with the other.

She had missed this. Being cut off and out-of-touch didn't suit her. And after replying to messages from her mother, Nikki, Carla (who was her oldest and dearest friend), several other mates, and blocking an ex who had contacted her out of the blue because he'd heard about her good fortune, Dulcie was searching for how to care for chickens when a familiar voice made her glance up from her screen.

The pub had filled up while she had been eating, but she spotted Otto immediately and stiffened. He was at the bar, talking to the landlord, and she was close enough to hear the conversation.

Not wanting Otto to notice her, she slumped in her seat, trying to hide behind the pepper grinder, and bent her head to her plate. Pretending to concentrate on her meal, she strained to hear what was being said as she peeped at him from underneath her lashes, enjoying being able to study him without him being aware of her scrutiny.

Otto might be an insufferable jerk, but he was a very good-looking and quite charismatic insufferable jerk, and she found she couldn't take her eyes off him. He was tall, with broad shoulders which tapered down to a slim waist and a nice bum, but it wasn't his physique that held her attention – it was his profile. Aquiline nose, full lips (but not too full), dark hair curling at the nape of his neck, hazel eyes, and even from this distance she could see how ridiculously long his lashes were. He looked different now though, and it took her a moment to realise what it was – he seemed to be uncomfortable and embarrassed, and she soon understood why when she stopped ogling him and tuned into the conversation.

He was asking the landlord for a job.

'I can't afford the likes of you,' the landlord said, 'even if I was looking for a chef. Which I'm not.'

Otto pulled a face. 'I wouldn't expect London wages, Dave.'

'All the same, my customers prefer pie and mash, not bits of this and dribbles of that served on a piece of slate or a dustbin lid.'

'I can cook pie and mash, you know,' Otto said, but he must have seen that he wasn't going to get anywhere, because he added, 'Look, keep me in mind, yeah?'

'I will, but by the time anything comes up, you'll probably be long gone.'

'I doubt that.' Otto slapped a hand on the bar. 'Thanks, Dave. It was worth a shot.'

'Good luck,' the landlord called after him as he left, and Dulcie wondered what all that was about.

Why would Otto, who was obviously well off and could afford a big fancy car and expensive clothes, and who could also afford to raffle off an entire farm for charity, be wanting to work in a small village pub?

She ate the rest of her meal with all kinds of thoughts whirling around her head, and when Dave came to collect her plate and ask whether she wanted to see the dessert menu, she said, 'Did I hear you say you've got a chef's job going?

'Eh?' He frowned, then his face cleared. 'Do you mean Otto York? No, I was telling him the exact opposite. Anyway, he's too upmarket for me.'

'In what way?' Curiosity was getting the better of her, and she knew she shouldn't be so nosey but she couldn't help it.

'He's one of those Michelin star chefs, and although I wouldn't mind a star or two, folk come here for good honest grub and plenty of it. If I started serving three peas on a plate with a splash of jus, I'd have a mutiny on my hands.'

'Otto is a **chef?**' Dulcie had assumed she must have heard wrong, but she was amazed to discover that she hadn't. She would never, in a million years, have guessed that Otto was a chef.

'He's a darned good one by all accounts, and a bit of a celebrity too,' Dave said. 'Now, can I interest you in some pudding?

The special today is white chocolate cheesecake with raspberries.'

'That sounds lovely,' she said, her fingers itching to start Googling, and she reached for her phone as soon as the landlord walked away.

'Otto Yok, Otto York,' she mumbled under her breath as she typed, then sat back, astounded, when she saw the number of hits his name generated. She clicked on the first, read it eagerly, then moved onto the next, and the one after that.

Otto York was indeed a chef. A well-known, well-respected chef, who ran his own kitchen in a prominent London restaurant. One that she would never be able to afford to eat in, even if she lived to be a hundred and started saving now.

She zoomed in on one of the many photos of him and studied his face. Then she turned her attention to the woman who was draped over him. She was gorgeous. As were the other women he had been photographed with. It seemed that Otto York liked to work hard and play hard, and although he didn't appear to have settled down with any of them, speculation was rife.

She also learned that he was thirty-four and loved hiking, dogs and the cinema.

But none of what she read was able to explain why a guy like him would be touting for work in a pub like The Black Horse.

Despite not wanting anything to do with the man, Dulcie was forced to admit that she was intrigued. And attracted. Let's not forget **attracted.**

CHAPTER FIVE

Broadband, finally! It had only taken six days, Dulcie thought sarcastically, as she checked her phone and noticed with relief that it was still connected to the router which had arrived yesterday. Thank goodness she had booked a whole week off work, guessing that she would have some sorting out to do. **Some?** Huh! She might have anticipated doing a spot of redecorating to make the place feel like hers, but she hadn't expected that she would need to strip the wallpaper from every single room, or that she would need a new kitchen, bathroom, downstairs loo, and flooring. The windows weren't the best and neither was the front door, or the back, but all Dulcie could do for the time being was to make it as cosy as possible with the limited funds she had at her disposal – which meant endless painting and a great deal of elbow grease.

She had decided to tackle the room that she'd designated to be the dining room first, as she was also going to be using it as an office and would therefore be spending most of her time in there when she started back to work on Monday. But it was Friday already, and she didn't feel as though she had made a great deal of headway, despite having worked on it all day for the past few days. She was exhausted, her body ached, her hands bore an uncanny resemblance to chickens' feet because they were so dry and chapped, and she had lived in grimy paint-spattered clothes for what seemed like forever.

She was determined to have a long hot shower later, style her hair, put some make-up on and head for the bright lights of Picklewick this evening, but before she could do that she had another full day of decorating ahead, so after she'd fed the chickens and fed herself, she continued with her painting.

Aside from all the decorating, Dulcie was beginning to feel like a proper farmer because she had made a truce with the chickens. Her newly-purchased wellies were responsible for that: with a sturdy rubber barrier between her ankles and their pecky beaks, she had felt brave enough to call them into their coop each evening, a structure which she had eventually found in the orchard. Her internet research had advised her that the easiest way to get a chicken to do what you wanted it to do was to bribe it with food, and she found that she quite enjoyed rattling pellets in a tin bucket and seeing them come running for their supper. And in turn, she more often than not found three warm eggs when she went to let them out the following morning. They didn't half whiff though – the chickens, not the eggs – and she was dreading having to clean out their little house. It was a task she was putting off until she felt brave enough. Maybe she could persuade her nephew to do it, if Nikki brought him for a visit at half term.

Suddenly a pang of homesickness and loneliness twanged her insides, and she put her paintbrush down. She missed her family, damn it, even though they were often annoying and chaotic.

None of them had ever lived in each other's pockets, having their own busy lives to lead, and she sometimes went weeks without seeing any of her siblings, although she often used to call in to see her mum. But this was different, and it abruptly struck her that apart from Otto, who she hadn't seen for several days, the only people she had spoken to face-to-face were shopkeepers, the pub's landlord and the postman. It spoke volumes when the highlight of her social calendar was hearing his van trundle up the hill. Yesterday he had brought her a very welcome card from Carla, wishing her all the best in her new home. As soon as she was settled, she would invite her for a visit, Dulcie vowed.

Just as the thought of the postman crossed her mind, there was a knock on the door and she stifled a surprised squeak. She hadn't heard the sound of an engine and it was a bit early, but her spirits lifted just the same, even though Ashton (yeah, she was on first-name terms with the guy) had mostly only brought her bills or junk mail. At least she was able to enjoy a few brief seconds of contact with another human being. She had caught herself talking to the chickens yesterday, and she had even tried to befriend the aloof ginger cat. All he had done was eye her with disdain and turn his back on her.

However, when she opened the door it wasn't the postman standing on her step. It was a woman with a baby on her hip and a wicker basket on her arm. Dulcie estimated her to be a couple of years older than herself, and she thought how pretty she was.

'Er, hello,' Dulcie said hesitantly.

'I'm Petra,' the woman said, 'and this little monster is Amory. We live at the stables, and we thought we'd better come and say hello. How are you settling in? Here, this is for you.' She offered Dulcie the basket and Dulcie took it, bemused. 'We would have said hi sooner, but we're converting an old feed store into a bungalow, and what with the builders, the horses, and this guy—' she jiggled the infant '—I've not had two minutes to myself. There's a cake in there, and some chutney, as well as a loaf of homemade bread.'

'I'm Dulcie. Thank you *so* much for this. I was about to put the kettle on. Have you got time for a cup of tea? Or coffee?'

'I certainly have,' the woman said, and Dulcie showed her in, leading her through the half-decorated dining room and into the kitchen.

'Sorry about the mess,' she said, feeling embarrassed about the state of the place.

'What mess?' Petra was gazing around curiously. 'It looks fine to me.'

Dulcie guessed that the woman was simply being polite, then was certain that she was when Petra added, 'You ought to see my kitchen. At least you haven't got a couple of dogs and a cat taking up floor space. Or toys everywhere.'

'It's a bit old-fashioned,' Dulcie said, lifting a pair of mugs off the mug tree and feeling thankful that she had washed up her breakfast things.

'I think your kitchen is quaint, and quite in keeping with the age of the house. A lick of paint and some new curtains on the windows and it'll be totally Instagram worthy.'

'Do you think so?'

Petra nodded. She had taken a seat at the scarred and pitted table that Dulcie had yet to transfer to the dining room, and was bouncing the baby on her knee. 'People love this kind of thing. I think you've either got to go high-end with a place like this or stick to traditional. Besides, it's a working farm – or, it **was** – so you can't expect it to be steel, chrome and shiny white tiles. Are you planning to restock soon?'

'I'm sorry...?' Dulcie wasn't sure what she meant. She removed the tea towel which was draped over the contents of the basket and peered inside. 'This cake looks divine. Did you make it yourself?'

'I can't cook for toffee,' Petra replied cheerfully. 'Amos, my uncle, baked that. Although I dare say I'll have to learn when he moves into his bungalow. Unless I can persuade Harry, my husband, to take over kitchen duties, that is.'

'I don't like cooking much, either,' Dulcie confessed, then asked, 'What did you mean by restock?'

'Bring a new flock in. Thanks.' Petra accepted a slice of the cake which Dulcie had popped onto a plate and placed on the table, and deftly moved it out of the reach of grabbing hands. 'You can't have any of this, sunshine,' she said to the baby, who waved his plump little arms in the air and blew a raspberry.

'A flock of what? Hens? I seem to have inherited three and that's more than enough, thanks.' Three she could cope with: any more would freak her out.

'I was talking about sheep. This is prime sheep rearing country, especially with the farm having grazing rights on the hillside.'

Dulcie shook her head vehemently. 'You've got to be joking! I was attacked by one the other day. It tried to get in the house, too. Horrid things.'

Petra laughed. 'I bet that was Flossie, Walter's lamb. She keeps turning up at the stables.'

'Walter should keep it locked up,' Dulcie said. 'It could do someone a serious injury.' By someone, she was referring to herself. 'And it's not like any lamb I've ever seen – it's **huge.**'

'She's a year old now,' Petra said, 'but she still thinks she's a baby. She's very docile. I expect she wanted a bottle. Walter hand-reared her last spring. Congratulations on winning the farm, by the way. We were all shocked when we found out that's what he and Otto were planning on doing with it.'

Dulcie slid onto a chair and bit into her cake. 'Oh. My. God. This is delicious.'

'I know.' Petra beamed at her.

When she swallowed her mouthful, Dulcie said, 'What's the story behind raffling the farm off? I mean, I'm all for giving money to charity, but *a* **whole farm?** I'm confused – I originally thought Otto was the owner, but he said it belonged to his dad.'

'You've met the delectable Otto?'

'He handed the keys over. He also told me off for leaving the chickens out overnight, and he rescued me from the sheep.' Dulcie blushed furiously as she remembered their previous encounter when she had ordered him off her property.

She caught Petra's eye and her blush deepened when she realised the woman was gazing at her thoughtfully.

'We didn't get off on the best foot,' Dulcie explained.

'He's gorgeous though, isn't he?' Petra said.

'And he knows it,' Dulcie retorted sharply. 'He's also rude and obnoxious.'

'Is he? I hadn't noticed. But then again, I can be rude and obnoxious myself. He's had a bit of a tough time lately,' Petra added. She drank the last of her tea and put the empty mug on the table. 'Right then, we'd better get a move on,' she said, getting to her feet. 'I've got a couple of welcome baskets to prepare for tomorrow. We rent out holiday cottages and there's always something that needs doing. Good luck with the decorating. You know where we are if you need us.'

Thanks,' Dulcie said, returning the basket to her. 'It was very kind of you.'

'It's nice to see a fresh face at Lilac Tree Farm,' Petra said. 'It was starting to look very sorry for itself.'

Dulcie walked her to the door, and just as Petra was about to leave, the woman said, 'Otto's not so bad, you know. If you give him a chance, you might find you like him.'

The problem was, Dulcie liked him already. Far too much, and not in the way Petra meant!

'Come on, Peg, let's stretch our legs.' Otto clicked his fingers and the sheepdog went to him, her tail wagging. 'You must miss being out on the hillside,' he said to her, as he fetched his coat and slipped it on. It was sunny outside and relatively warm, but he knew how quickly the weather could change, and it was still too early in the year not to wear a coat. If he got too hot, he could always take it off.

'Dad, I'm taking Peg out for a couple of hours. Will you be alright on your own?'

'Silly beggar, of course I will be. I'm not an invalid.'

No, his dad wasn't, but he wasn't as well as he might be, either, and Otto continued to be concerned about him. Thankfully, Walter was a little better than he had been when Otto had paid him that surprise visit at the start of the year. The visit that had changed everything. Otto acutely recalled how appalled he had felt when he saw his father, and how worried he had been that he was going to lose him.

Otto blamed himself.

But he was here now, and he was caring for his dad to the best of his ability, even when his father seriously objected to it. Thankfully, with the awful strain he had been under now lifting, his dad was starting to look and behave more like his old self.

Unable to imagine what his dad had been going through, having to borrow from Peter to pay Paul to keep the farm afloat, Otto was still cross that Walter hadn't confided in him sooner, before the debts had escalated to such an extent that saving the farm was an impossibility.

He sighed as he started walking up the lane. It was water under the bridge. What was done, was done, and there was no point in wailing about it. All he could do was make the best of it, look to the future and not dwell on the past. However, he still felt like the worst son in the world for not realising how bad things had become.

Pushing such non-productive thoughts out of his mind, Otto turned his attention to what he could do going forward. He had been mulling it over a lot lately, but so far he had hit a brick wall.

He had approached every restaurant, pub and cafe within a realistic commuting distance from Muddypuddle Cottage, with absolutely no luck whatsoever. No one was hiring a chef, although he had seen some vacancies for bar and waiting staff. If push came to shove and his savings ran out, he might well have to go down that route, even though it would be hell being so near to a commercial kitchen, when all he would be allowed to do was serve the meals.

Deep down he was still hoping to be able to return to London at some point, because that was where most of the job opportunities lay. He had worked so incredibly hard to get where he was, yet in a few short months he was almost back to where he had started.

Not quite, because he had the experience, the skill and his reputation to fall back on, but the world of professional cheffing was a hard and cut-throat one, and out of sight often meant out of mind. And living in Picklewick was as out of sight as it was possible to get.

The view was good though, he thought glumly, as he turned to face down the hill and scanned the valley below. He had missed this, he realised, drinking in the view. Every field was emerald with new growth, and the hedgerows were lush and leaf covered. The bleat of sheep and their lambs carried on the warm air, and a pang of regret hit him. It might be a very long time indeed until their cries were heard once more on the farm on Muddypuddle Lane. If ever.

The fields were already turning into meadow, now that they were no longer being grazed, and Otto spotted the white petals of oxeye daisies with their bright yellow centres, and the pinky-purple flowers of red clover and mallow could be seeing blooming in the long grass. The bees were having a great time, and he spotted so many fat bumbles that he lost count. A red kite circled overhead, its cry wild and savage, and he realised that nature was beginning to reclaim what was rightfully hers.

It was a sight that was probably replicated all over Britain, as farms went out of business – he forgot how many farmers a year packed it in or went bankrupt, but it was a lot. And the chances of his farm ever being used again for its intended purpose were remote. The best Otto could hope for was that a family would love it and grow up in it, and that the place wouldn't undergo any drastic changes in the process. But he had his doubts that the new owner would see the character in the old beams, the beauty of the grey flagstones on the floor that had been polished to a sheen by the passage of many feet, or the history in the bare stone walls of the sitting room. No doubt she would modernise it to within an inch of its life, until it looked exactly like any other house.

He had debated whether to walk up the lane because that meant he would have to go right past the house he used to call home. He could just have easily taken the path opposite the stables which would have taken him to the top of the hill albeit in a more roundabout and less steep route. But he had to get used to the stark reality that the farm was no longer in his family.

Telling himself to toughen up, Otto plodded up the lane and turned his attention back to what he was going to do with himself for the foreseeable future.

Otto didn't do idleness. He was far too restless a person to relax and twiddle his thumbs, and there was only so much cleaning, laundry and dog walking to be done. There was also a limit to the amount of cooking he could do. Three meals a day for two people was hardly going to keep him occupied for long, especially since his dad was dropping subtle hints that a three-course breakfast wasn't strictly necessary, and please could he have something simple like eggs, beans and chips for tea one night. 'And none of those triple-cooked chips, neither,' he had added.

But without cooking, without spending his days in a kitchen and creating wonderful food, Otto was nothing.

He took a deep lungful of clean spring air, trying to blow away the sadness invading his mind, and sniffed appreciatively as a familiar smell shot up his nose.

He had forgotten that wild garlic grew on the other side of the hedge, and when he came to a gap in the foliage, he peered through it to the pretty white flowers on the other side. There were loads of them, and he breathed deeply, wondering whether he should pick any of the edible blooms to add to the meal he would make tonight.

Then his spirits sank as he thought of the expression on his father's face if he saw flowers on his plate. He wouldn't be impressed, and would no doubt refuse to even try one.

Look, there was alexander, or horse parsley as it was also known, and it too was edible. And so were the new leaves of the brambles which scrambled over the dry stone wall. If you knew where to look, spring was an amazingly abundant time for foragers, and he remembered picking all kinds of things when he was a boy and taking them home to experiment with. He had loved cooking even when he was a kid—

Otto froze.

A thought was beginning to form, and it wasn't half bad...

Absently, he picked a hawthorn blossom and held it to his nose, inhaling its almondy scent. The tree was only just coming into flower, most of the buds still tightly furled, but one or two had braved the elements and were fully open. He picked a second, before popping them both into his mouth. The taste of marzipan exploded on his tongue, and he closed his eyes with pleasure. You can't get fresher than this, he thought.

'What are you doing?' a voice asked, and he opened them to find Dulcie watching him warily.

Instead of answering her question, he asked one of his own. 'Is there any chard or kale in the veggie patch?'

Dulcie pulled a face. 'I've no idea. I don't know what either of them look like.' And from her suspicious expression, she probably wouldn't tell him if she did, he concluded.

But she surprised him. 'Do you want to take a look?'

'If you don't mind.' He suddenly remembered that he had patient gentle Peg with him. 'Are you okay with dogs?'

She narrowed her eyes. 'I like dogs. They're cute. What's his name?'

'He is a she, and her name is Peg. She belongs to my dad.'

'She's a sheepdog, isn't she?'

She is, but she's retired now, since we've not got any sheep for her to work.'

'Except the one.'

'Ah, yes, Flossie.'

Dulcie walked over to the dog and crouched down, holding out her hand for her to sniff, which Peg obediently did, her tail wagging in greeting. 'The veggie patch is rather overgrown,' she said. 'I haven't had a chance to do anything with it.'

'It's been overgrown for a long time,' Otto replied, sadly. As his dad's health began to fail, he'd had to let some things go, and the veggie patch was one of them. Still, with a bit of TLC and a lot of graft, it could look as good as it had been in its heyday, when his mum had been in charge of it and the family had eaten fresh homegrown produce most of the year round.

Dulcie gave the dog a final pat and straightened up. 'Were you eating that tree?' She was eyeing him strangely again.

'I was,' he admitted. 'Hawthorn blossom is edible.'

'I'll take your word for it.' She didn't look convinced.

He reached out and plucked another flower. 'Try it.'

'Er, no thanks. Is that what you do in your restaurant? Cook weird stuff?'

Otto was surprised. He wasn't aware that she knew he was a chef. 'I don't cook weird stuff,' he retorted.

'Eating flowers is weird,' Dulcie shot back.

'Edible flowers are being used more and more in the kitchen,' he pointed out.

'Not in mine.'

He blinked. 'Are **you** a chef?' He wondered where she worked.

'**Me?** Good lord, no! I can just about make an omelette.'

'Oh, I thought...when you said...' He trailed off.

'You do realise that most people don't plonk daffodils on their dinner?' she pointed out.

'I'm pleased to hear it. Eating daffodils can make you quite unwell. I make sure I only incorporate edible flowers into my cooking.'

'I'm not sure I fancy it.' Dulcie looked sceptical, and vaguely revolted.

'I'm sure if you tried them, you would like them,' Otto insisted. He didn't know why he was trying to convince her, but if his vague idea of a hedgerow-to-plate cookbook was to stand any chance of getting off the ground, it would need to have a wide appeal. If he could convince someone like Dulcie – who openly admitted that she wasn't much of a cook – that eating foraged foods and the edible plants growing in their gardens was a good thing, then his idea might stand a chance.

'Tell you what,' he said. 'How about I cook you a meal made with fresh ingredients picked from the garden and the hedgerows? And you can give me your verdict.'

Her eyes widened. 'Um, okay.'

'How about this evening?' he suggested, eager to get started. 'Unless you've got plans?'

'No plans.'

'Great! See you later,' he said, excitement coursing through him.

But was he excited about finally getting back into the kitchen and trying out a new recipe or two on someone who wasn't his dad, or was he excited at the thought of seeing Dulcie again?

Stunned didn't begin to describe how Dulcie felt when Otto invited her to dinner. And it wasn't a going-to-the-pub dinner either – although she was sure that would have been lovely. This was a

Michelin star chef, cooking a meal just for her.

How special did **she** feel right now?!

She had spotted him from the window earlier, and had stopped work to watch him as he strolled up the hill. Her heart had missed a beat and the sudden lurch of excitement in her tummy had taken her by surprise.

It hadn't been her intention to go speak to him but her curiosity had been piqued when he began rooting around in the hedge, and she simply had to see what he was doing. Especially since she was pretty sure that the hedge he was molesting belonged to her.

And now, the great Otto York was going to cook a meal for little old Dulcie Fairfax! Her friends would be well-jealous. And so would her sisters. Maisie, especially, had been almost apoplectic with envy when she had told her (rather smugly) that she knew Otto York, and that he lived in the cottage on Muddypuddle Lane. She thought she might have had to hold Maisie back with a chair and whip to stop her from jumping on the train and coming to visit.

Dulcie hurried inside the house to grab her phone, excitement making her squeal, and she was about to make a few calls when she paused.

Maisie was model-pretty, highly-strung, flighty and dreamy. She and Otto would look good together, and with Maisie simpering all over him, how would he be able to resist her?

The thought made her bristle. Not that she didn't want Maisie to be happy (she

did) but when it came to Otto, Dulcie felt a bit dog-in-a-manger about him. She wasn't interested in him herself – god forbid, he was too arrogant and up himself – but that wasn't the point.

Actually, she wasn't sure what the point was, but there was bound to be one.

CHAPTER SIX

What to wear...? Dulcie was standing in her underwear in front of the large wardrobe and peering into its depths. She wanted to look nice, but not *too* nice. She was fairly sure this wasn't a date, so she didn't want to appear as though she was trying too hard, but she also didn't want to look as though she'd not made any effort at all. Because, let's face it, apart from the day when he'd handed her the keys to the farmhouse, Otto hadn't seen her looking her best. A cow onesie and scruffy paint-spattered work clothes didn't project the sort of image she would have liked.

Eventually, she settled on a pair of skinny black jeans, a top in the loveliest shade of aqua, a jacket in case it got chilly later, and a pair of ballet pumps. Although... maybe wearing such delicate shoes to walk down the lane wasn't the best idea.

She wished she had a bottle of wine to take with her, but having not gone shopping for a few days, there wasn't any left. Dulcie had drunk it all. She had taken to having a glass or two with her supper after she had downed tools for the day.

The thought of food made her tummy rumble. Apart from that one meal in The Black Horse, she had been living on soup, sandwiches and whatever ready meals she had in the freezer. And eggs, of course: she had plenty of eggs.

That was a thought! She could take him some eggs, and maybe pick some flowers.

Her garden had an abundance of tulips, she had noticed, and although it was more traditional for a man to give a woman flowers, considering he was going to feed her some of the damned things, she didn't think he would mind.

As she picked them, she did wonder if tulips were edible, and she was briefly tempted to eat one. She had even got as far as putting a brilliant orange-coloured flower to her lips before common sense slapped her on the cheek. Otto knew what he was doing – hopefully. Dulcie didn't. She hadn't even recognised spinach when Otto had pointed it out to her earlier, and she loved spinach. It had been a common ingredient in the food boxes which she had occasionally resorted to buying, during those times when she had vowed to become a better and more consistent cook, and not live off takeaways and ready meals.

After picking an armful of brightly coloured blooms, Dulcie stopped for a moment to enjoy the beauty of her new garden, and she took a deep breath of flower-scented air. There were no formal beds as such, just a riot of spring colour – the tulips were accompanied by a few late daffodils (although most of them were past their prime now), and she also recognised pansies, peonies and iris, and there was even a splendid lilac tree at the far end, marking the boundary between the garden and the vegetable plot. She guessed the farm must have been named after it, and even from this distance she could smell the sweet fragrance of its blossoms.

Dulcie suddenly realised how lucky she was to live in such a wonderful place. Of all the competitions she had entered over the years (and there had been many) she'd never won anything – but for her to have won not only a house, but a house in such a gorgeous location...

She felt very blessed indeed.

'Hi,' Otto said when he opened the door, and as he did so Dulcie handed him the flowers.

'These are for you,' she explained, feeling embarrassed and apologetic. 'I didn't have any wine, and I couldn't come empty-handed.'

'That's very thoughtful,' he said, taking them from her and burying his nose in the petals.

Dulcie's nose was far more concerned with the mouth-watering aroma of onions and garlic. And was that roast chicken she could smell? Her tummy rumbled loudly and she winced, hoping he hadn't heard.

'I brought some eggs, too,' she said. She had wrapped them in a tea towel, and she passed it to him. 'I'm getting a bit fed up of eggs,' she admitted. 'I feel I should use them, but I've run out of ideas of what to do with them. I suppose I could do some baking, but I've not got the time and neither am I very good at it.' She halted abruptly, realising that she was wittering. Not only that, she sounded as though she was dropping great big hints.

'I can give you a few ideas, if you like,' Otto offered.

'He's full of them,' a voice called from inside the cottage.

Otto grimaced. 'Sorry, where are my manners? Please, come in. I hope you like chicken? I forgot to ask if you're vegetarian.' He looked worried, as he caught his bottom lip between his teeth.

Dulcie's attention was drawn to his mouth, and she hastily dragged it away. 'I love chicken,' she enthused as he gestured for her to walk ahead of him, but disappointment bit her sharply on the backside when she realised they weren't to dine alone. An elderly gentleman was sitting in an armchair and peering at her over the top of his glasses.

'This is my dad, Walter. Dad, this is Dulcie. I'll put these in water,' Otto said, jerking his chin at the flowers. He had a nice chin...to go with his nice mouth.

Gah! What was wrong with her? She was here for a meal, nothing more. Clearly.

'So, you're the girl who won the farm,' Walter said.

Dulcie nodded and made a face, unsure what to say. She had a feeling there was more to raffling off the farm than she knew. She had asked Petra outright, but her neighbour hadn't given her an answer and Dulcie realised that she had deftly changed the subject, turning the conversation away from the farm and onto Otto himself.

'I trust you'll take good care of it.' Walter scowled at her.

'She will, Dad.' Otto had appeared in the doorway. 'Sit down Dulcie, you're making the place look untidy. Can I get you something to drink? Wine?'

'Wine would be lovely.'

'Will white be okay? It'll go better with the chicken.'

'Thanks.'

He went back into the kitchen, leaving Dulcie to smile awkwardly at his father.

'I used to have sheep. And chooks.' Walter was staring into the unlit fireplace with a wistful expression. She guessed him to be in his mid-seventies, and he looked frail and careworn, despite a weather-beaten face and rough calloused hands. He was rubbing them together, and she wondered if she was making him uncomfortable.

'The hens are still there,' she said.

Walter perked up. 'I thought Otto had got rid of all the livestock. How is Mable? She can be a bit flighty.'

'I've no idea, sorry.'

'No idea about what?' Otto appeared at her side. He was holding a large glass with a couple of inches of wine in the bottom.

'Which of the hens is which,' she said. 'I didn't even know my hens had names. I mean, Walter's hens.' Oh dear, she thought: she was in danger of putting her foot in it. 'Would you like them back?'

She would be more than happy for someone to take them off her hands. She might have come to accept them, but that didn't mean to say she **liked** them. Even the novelty of fresh eggs every morning had quickly worn off.

'They're better off staying at the farm for the time being,' Otto said. 'Maybe when we're a bit more sorted.' He shot his father a concerned glance. 'We've got enough with Flossie and Peg, haven't we, Dad?'

Walter didn't look convinced.

'You can come and visit them if you want,' Dulcie offered. 'And you can tell me their names.'

He scratched his chin. 'Their names are Mable, Dolly and Lucky. They probably saw the sheep being rounded up and thought they were for the chop, so they gave my son the slip.'

Dulcie was horrified. 'They weren't...' She hesitated to say it, and suddenly the smell of roast chicken didn't seem quite so appetising.

'Nah, they were good layers. You don't give a good layer the chop unless it stops laying. How many eggs are you getting?'

'Three a day, every day,' Dulcie said.

'They must like you. Chickens can be a bit pernickety.'

Despite not being all that keen on them, being told that the hens must like her gave Dulcie a warm glow, and she felt an urge to know which was which. Mind you, even if Walter did point out Mabel from Dolly, Dulcie still didn't think she would be able to tell one from the other. All three were brown, clucky and feathery.

'If you'd like to take a seat at the table,' Otto called, 'dinner is served.

Dulcie hadn't known what she had been expecting – a kitchen very much like her own, perhaps – but when she entered this one it was very different. Although small and galley-shaped, it had two rows of sleek glossy cabinets on either side, and a large oven that seemed to be the focal point. At the far end, near the door to the garden, was a small round table with four chairs. It had been laid with a pristine white tablecloth and gleaming cutlery.

'What are you trying to poison us with today?' Walter asked, as he shuffled into his seat. 'He's a chef, you know. Likes drizzles of this and soupçons of that.'

Otto shot his father an amused look. 'Dad is getting fed up with my fancy cooking,' he said. 'I think he has a hankering for simpler things, like beans on toast.' Otto shuddered.

'Don't knock it,' Dulcie said. 'There's a time and a place for beans on toast.'

'Not you as well.' Otto sighed dramatically, but there was an indulgent look in his eye and Dulcie couldn't help wondering whether this was the same grumpy, unfriendly man who she had met on her first day, the same one who had told her off about the chickens.

She rather liked this new updated version. He was just as handsome, but he was now beginning to develop the personality to complement his good looks. Or maybe that personality had been there all along, but she had brought out the worst in him?

Otto placed a bowl of soup in front of her. It was green, with a swirl of what she thought might be cream on top. A small roll sat on her side plate, warm to the touch, and curls of yellow butter lay on a dish in the centre of the table.

'Sorrel soup,' Otto said, serving his dad before he sat down himself, then he picked up his spoon. He made no move to dip it in the soup, though. He was too busy watching her.

She took a cautious sip.

A burst of flavour exploded on her tongue, delicate, fresh and considerably moreish. She ate another spoonful.

Otto continued to study her.

'Well?' he asked eventually. He still hadn't touched his. Walter, on the other hand, was hoovering his up, despite his insistence that he didn't want any more fancy food.

'It's really, really nice,' Dulcie enthused. 'Sorrell, you said? Did you pick it from my garden?'

She winced as she saw a shadow flit across his face, and she realised how hard it must be for him to accept that his dad's property now belonged to her. Dulcie pursed her lips, but they didn't stay pursed for long because she simply had to eat the rest of her soup.

'Yep, freshly picked today,' he said, his voice light, making Dulcie wonder if she'd imagined it.

She tore into her roll, releasing a warm bready smell, and reached for the butter, wanting to taste everything Otto had to offer.

The bread was just as delicious as the soup.

'Did you get these rolls from the village?' she asked, thinking she would buy some the next time she was in Picklewick.

Otto gave her a bemused look. 'I baked them myself.'

Of course he did, she thought. 'Don't tell me you made the butter as well?'

He chuckled, a sound that sent a delicious shiver through her. It was throaty and sexy, and abruptly she didn't want to taste any more of his food – she wanted to taste *him*.

Dulcie put down the roll she was nibbling on, her appetite for food suddenly gone, replaced with an altogether different kind of appetite.

My, my, she had better put a stop to this unwanted desire: nothing good would come of it.

'I didn't make the butter,' Otto admitted, 'although I will make some next time, if you like.'

Next time?

Dulcie resisted the urge to fan herself with her hands. Did he mean that he wanted to see her again, or that he wanted to try out some more dishes on her? Either way, sexy man plus sexy food was a heady combination. No wonder women were attracted to him.

Was he as passionate in bed as he was about his cooking?

The thought made her head spin.

Oh, man, she needed to get out more. A week on the farm with only herself and three chickens for company was taking its toll. She needed to start making some new friends – fast.

Dulcie realised she had finished the soup and the roll, her hands and mouth on automatic pilot whilst her mind had been otherwise engaged.

'Not bad, that,' Walter announced, dropping his spoon into his bowl with a clatter. 'Mind, you can't beat a tin of Heinz tomato,' he added.

Dulcie's eyes widened, and then she noticed the twinkle in the elderly man's eye.

Otto shook his head, an indulgent smile on those gorgeous lips of his.

'Just pulling your leg, son,' Walter said. He turned to Dulcie and winked.

'Ready for your mains?' Otto asked, rolling his eyes and making Dulcie giggle.

'Definitely. What is it?' she asked.

'Roast chicken with wild-garlic potatoes, and a salad of chickweed, spinach, hawthorn buds and leaves, lime leaves, and red clover to garnish.'

'What's that?' Walter asked, pointing at the deep red liquid that Otto was pouring sparingly over the crispy golden chicken. 'See, drizzle this, jus that,' the old man grumbled.

'Blackberry ju— **sauce**,' Otto replied. 'I didn't pick those today, obviously, but I thought the chicken needed a little something. In an ideal world, I would have picked them last autumn and frozen them, but I bought them from the greengrocer in the village instead.'

'I don't care where you got them,' Dulcie told him when she tasted it, and she closed her eyes in bliss as she chewed. She had expected him to be a damned good cook, but not **this** good.

She opened them again to find him gazing at her and she blushed, hastily swallowing her mouthful.

Her mouth suddenly dry, she sipped at her wine. For a moment there, she thought she had seen something in his eyes...

Shaking the thought off, she tried to concentrate on her food, but as she ate, her gaze kept returning to Otto, and each time it did she found him looking at her. And each time he would give a little smile and look away.

By the time dessert was ready to be served, Dulcie was completely out of sorts. She didn't think she had ever been so acutely aware of a man. The way he'd rolled up his sleeves to reveal the dark hairs on his forearms. His long fingers with their neatly trimmed nails. The muscles in his upper arms. The way his hair curled ever so slightly at the back of his neck. She wanted to touch it, to see if those curls were as soft as they looked.

As he stirred something in a pan, she studied the outline of his jaw, the slope of his nose, the shape of his mouth when he quickly dipped a teaspoon in the pan and tasted what he was making. He licked his lips, and her insides fizzed as she imagined what it would be like to be kissed by him.

Take a breath, lady, she told herself: it's not you he's interested in, it's your opinion of his food that he's after.

And this was borne out when he watched her tuck into a generous slice of dandelion cake with gorse flower syrup. It was divine, and her appreciation must have shown on her face because he beamed when he saw her reaction.

'Would you eat it again?' he asked.

'Definitely!' Dulcie was emphatic.

'Is there anything about this menu that you didn't like?'

'Nothing. I enjoyed every mouthful. Who knew weeds could be so delicious?'

Otto sat back. 'That's a relief.'

She narrowed her eyes. 'Why?' Something in his tone made her think there had been more to this meal than simply trying to justify his hedgerow nibbling.

'I'm thinking of writing a book of foraging recipes,' Otto announced.

Walter said, 'You are? Since when?'

'Since this morning. I miss being in the kitchen and I've got to do something with my time, so...'

'So, go back to London,' Walter said. 'Now the farm has been sorted, there's no need for you to stay here. I can manage on my own.'

'I know you can,' Otto said, getting to his feet and collecting up the empty plates. 'But I thought I would stick around for a bit longer. I've been wanting to write a cookbook for a while, but I wanted it to be different. I just didn't know how.'

'Until today?' Walter said.

'Until today,' Otto agreed. 'You can blame Dulcie.'

'Me?' Dulcie gasped.

Otto chuckled. 'She caught me eating hawthorn blossom earlier. You ought to have seen the look on her face.'

'Is **that** why you invited her to dinner?' Walter asked. 'I thought it might be because—'

'Can I top up your glass?' Otto interrupted, looking at Dulcie.

'Go on, then,' she said, holding it out to him.

'Would you like some more wine, Dad?'

'Not for me. I'd love a nice cup of tea, though.'

'Go into the sitting room and I'll bring you one in,' Otto instructed.

He watched his dad leave and there was silence for a moment. Dulcie could see the concern in his eyes, and she wondered whether he was worried about his father and if that was the reason why he was staying in Picklewick. She also recalled him touting for work, and she guessed he must be desperate for a job. Why else would such a fantastic chef want to work in a small village out in the sticks? She shook her head as she remembered her initial thoughts on the first day. He might have a big car, and he might dress well, but he didn't appear to be any better off financially than she was.

Her heart went out to him. No wonder he had been so grumpy – he had a lot on his plate.

Ah, plates...

'Let me help with the washing up,' she offered.

'Not a chance. You're a guest.'

'And a sounding board?' she asked.

'That, too,' he admitted, plunging his hands into hot soapy water.

'Are you really going to write a book?'

'I'm thinking about it.'

'I'm no food critic, but if you want a guinea pig I'll give you my honest opinion. And what you cooked this evening was heavenly.' She realised she wasn't making this offer solely because he served wonderful food: it was because it would be an excuse to see him again.

'Eating flowers and leaves wasn't that bad, was it?' he teased.

She noticed that he hadn't said he would take her up on her offer. 'They were just about edible,' she smirked.

'Would you cook any of the dishes you ate this evening?' he asked.

'No way!'

'Oh. Too complicated? Too radical?' His face fell, and Dulcie felt sorry for him.

'Too...cooky. I don't cook much, to be honest.'

'When you do, what do you like to cook?'

Dulcie shrugged. 'Omelette, mac-n-cheese, soup.' She was also a fan of Pot Noodles, but she wasn't going to admit that to a top-notch chef.

'Making soup is cooking,' he pointed out.

'Not when it comes out of a tin or a plastic tub,' she said ruefully. She occasionally treated herself to a soup out of the supermarket chiller section, rather than open a tin, and that was the closest she came to home-made soup.

They chatted about food as Otto cleaned up, Dulcie sipping her wine, and when the kitchen was tidy and the only reminder of the fabulous meal she had just eaten was a faint aroma in the air, Dulcie thanked him and prepared to leave.

'I'll walk you back up the hill,' Otto said.

'There's no need. I can find my own way home.' Although she would love him to, she didn't want him to feel obliged.

'I want to.' He gazed into her eyes and her heart fluttered.

Oh my, he wanted to escort her back to the farm. Maybe he didn't want the evening to end just yet, either.

But she was quickly brought back to earth when he added, 'It's dark out and I don't want you twisting an ankle in one of those potholes.'

Oh. That's what he meant. He was just being chivalrous.

'They are rather impressive,' she said lightly, to cover her disappointment as she walked through the living room and headed towards the door. 'Bye, Walter. It was lovely meeting you.'

'You, too. Be careful going up the lane.'

'I'm going with her,' Otto said.

Dulcie almost missed the satisfaction on the old man's face and the warning look on Otto's, and she wondered what that was all about, but when they stepped outside, she forgot about it as she turned her face up to the sky.

'I've never seen so many stars!' she exclaimed.

'It helps that there isn't a moon tonight,' Otto said. 'Which is another reason I wanted to escort you home. I bet you didn't think to bring a torch with you.'

'I don't actually own one. I'd better add it to my shopping list.'

'There's one in the feed store,' he said. 'It might still work.'

'Your dad left quite a bit of stuff behind when he moved out.'

They began to walk up the hill, their pace little more than a dawdle. It was very quiet, she realised. There was hardly a breath of air to stir the leaves in the hedgerow, although she could hear the occasional rustle of an animal in the undergrowth, and she was glad Otto had insisted on accompanying her.

Otto sighed. 'You've seen how small Muddypuddle Cottage is. He couldn't bring much with him. I did think of emptying the place, but you know what farmers are like – they never get rid of anything in case it might come in handy, and there was just so much of it. I suppose I could have called in a company to clear the house, but as for the barns and the sheds...' He trailed off.

'If you don't mind me asking, why didn't you sell the farm? Why did you raffle it?' She couldn't shake the feeling that his finances were little better than her own. The cottage was much smaller than the farmhouse, although she could tell that it had recently had work done on it, especially the kitchen. And if he was as well off as she had initially assumed, why had he asked the landlord of The Black Horse for a job?

'I tried, but...' He shrugged. 'I might as well tell you because everyone in the village knows – my dad was up to his neck in debt. We had no choice but to raffle it.'

Dulcie was even more confused. 'I don't understand.'

'What he would have got if he had sold it, wouldn't have covered his debts. No one wants to buy a hill farm these days. Farming is bloody hard work and farms are going out of business left, right and centre. There's no money in it. That's why you see so many of them diversifying. We did consider alternatives such as glamping, but we couldn't afford the initial outlay.'

'But you just **gave** it away?' Dulcie had a sudden terrifying thought that as the new owner of the farm *she* might be responsible for those debts.

'It wasn't a raffle, as such. It was a lottery, and the money raised from selling tickets was enough to pay off my dad's debts, with a decent amount left over to give to charity.'

'You gave the rest to **charity?**' Gosh, what a hero. Dulcie didn't think she would have been as generous.

'That was one of the conditions for running the lottery – all proceeds have to go to charity, less certain expenses. For other companies who run this kind of thing, that would usually include the purchase of the property itself. In Dad's case, we were able to pay off the mortgage and everything else.' Otto tilted his head back to look at the heavens. 'It was a shame it had to end like this, but I couldn't see any other way out. Anyway, Dad's health isn't the best, so he couldn't have continued to run the farm for much longer.'

'Did you not want to run it yourself?' They had almost reached the entrance to the farmyard, and she slowed, not wanting the conversation to end.

'Cheffing is my thing,' he said. 'It always has been. I've never wanted to do anything else, and you can't be a chef the way I wanted to be a chef, and run a farm at the same time.'

They came to a halt outside her front door. Should she ask him in? She wanted to, but what if he declined? She would feel like a proper idiot. But on the other hand, if he agreed, he might get the wrong idea. She didn't want the evening to end, but neither did she have any intention of jumping into bed with him, not after seeing the women he had been photographed with. Although she might fancy him like crazy, Dulcie had more self-respect than to become another notch on his bedpost. Saying that though, he hadn't shown the slightest interest in her in that way, so she was probably overthinking things.

'Thanks for walking me up the hill,' she said, turning to face him and digging around in her jacket pocket for her keys.

'You're welcome.'

'And thanks for a lovely meal. It was astounding.'

'I'm so pleased you enjoyed it.'

Otto smiled, and Dulcie hastily averted her gaze from his gorgeous lips, and nibbled at her own, catching the bottom one between her teeth as she resisted the urge to stand on tiptoe and kiss him.

She cleared her throat. 'Thanks again, and if you want a guinea pig for any more recipes, I'm your gal!' she reminded him.

'You might regret saying that,' he joked. 'Goodnight.'

'Goodnight,' Dulcie replied, but he had already begun to walk away and he raised his hand, waving without turning around.

Yep, it was as she had surmised – he was only interested in her for her tastebuds.

CHAPTER SEVEN

'There's something sexy about a man cooking for you,' Nikki observed, when Dulcie phoned her the following morning. She simply couldn't keep it to herself, and her sensible, level-headed sister was the person she chose to call.

She could have had a chat with any number of her friends, and Carla should have been the obvious choice, but Dulcie wanted to keep her growing feelings for this man in-house, so to speak. Carla was flighty and flirty, and didn't believe in love or relationships, and as Dulcie had never seen her fall for a guy, she wasn't sure Carla would understand how Dulcie was feeling. Heck, Dulcie herself didn't understand.

She'd had relationships in the past, some of them fairly serious, but none of them had amounted to more than a few wasted months of her life and a bruised heart.

But this felt different. More grown up.

It might be because she was rapidly approaching thirty (she had a year or so to go yet, but she was aware it was looming) or it might be because she was finally a homeowner. It might even be because she had no family or friends in her immediate vicinity to fall back on. But whatever the reason, she had never felt like this before. And the daft thing was, she hardly knew him.

Dulcie wasn't an insta-love kind of girl. She took her time to get to know a fella before she let her emotions loose on him. She might be ditzy in other ways (not as ditzy as Maisie, thankfully – but then *no one* was as ditzy as her younger sister). In ways such as freaking out over a chicken, for instance, but when it came to matters of the heart she was cautious to the point of being accused of not having a heart at all.

She definitely did have one, but having seen the way Maisie fell in and out of love at the drop of a hat, Dulcie had no intention of doing the same. Maisie lived her life on a roller-coaster of emotions, either madly in love, or in floods of tears and heartbroken. It must be exhausting.

On the other side of the coin was Nikki – divorced with an eleven-year-old son. She had only ever loved one man and look how that had turned out! Dulcie had been serious when she had offered to beat Nikki's lying, cheating husband over the head with a shovel, then use that same shovel to bury him.

Okay, maybe not really serious, because she never would have gone through with it, but imagining doing away with her rotten brother-in-law had helped her cope with Nikki's distress, during her sister's darker moments.

'Dulcie, are you still there?' Nikki asked.

'Huh? Oh, yeah, sorry.' Dulcie refocused. 'It *was* sexy, despite his dad being there.'

'His **dad?**' Nikki spluttered, her laughter carrying over the airwaves.

'Yeah, he lives with him in a cottage down the lane. It was originally part of the farm, but they hung on to it.'

'You're going gaga over a guy who still lives at home with his **dad?**'

'It's not like that,' Dulcie protested and she went on to explain the situation.

Nikki said in a more sober voice, 'What did you say his name was?'

'Otto York.'

'**The** Otto York? The chef? Why didn't you say so! He's famous. When can I come for a visit? Do you think he'll cook for me, too?'

'You sound like Maisie,' Dulcie grumbled. 'This is why I didn't say anything sooner. I know what you lot are like. Don't tell Mum or Maisie,' she warned. 'They'll be here in a flash, and I've got loads of decorating to do.'

'Mum could help with that,' Nikki said. 'And I'm definitely coming to visit you at half term. I'm dying to see the place. It looks idyllic.'

Dulcie had sent loads of pictures to her family – carefully crafted photos which displayed the farm in the best possible light. The reality was rather different, but she was hoping that by the time her family descended on her, the interior of the house would look the best she could make it with the resources and funds she had available.

'Sorry,' she said, hearing a knock. 'I've got to go, there's someone at the door.'

Dulcie hurried to the front door, her heart pitter-pattering in the hope that it might be Otto. She had to hide her disappointment when she realised her visitor was Petra.

'Hi,' Dulcie greeted her, warmly. 'Come in.'

'I'd love to, but I can't stop. I just wondered if you'd like to come to The Black Horse tonight? It's Lena's birthday.'

'Um...'

'Sorry, you don't have any idea who Lena is, do you? She's my uncle's girlfriend – soon to be partner when they move in together. I just thought it might be nice for you to pop along and meet some people. We don't bite, honest. If you didn't want to drive, you can come in the Land Rover with us.' Petra's eyes flickered sideways to Dulcie's game little hatchback.

'That would be lovely,' Dulcie said. 'Thanks.'

Her spirits soared as she thought about the evening ahead. It was so nice of Petra to invite her, and she wondered what to take as a gift, because she couldn't arrive empty-handed.

Skipping the decorating for today, Dulcie decided to subject her poor car to the perils of Muddypuddle Lane, and pop into the village. After all, it was Saturday and she had earned a day off, and with the prospect of an evening in the pub, she was in no mood to do any more damned painting!

'This is Charity and her partner, Timothy. He's Harry's brother and one of the vets at Picklewick Veterinary Practice. She works at the care home in the village and also helps out at the stables. She's got a twin sister Faith, who—'

Dulcie's eyes glazed over. The girl waving at her was the umpteenth person she had been introduced to so far this evening, and there was no way she was going to remember all their names, let alone figure out who was connected to who. She was okay with Harry, Petra's husband, because he had driven them to the pub, and she also remembered the baby's name. She thought Amos might be the old guy, who was sitting next to the lady whose birthday it was, but as for the rest...there were just too many of them.

Everyone was gathered around several tables that had been pushed together, and all of them seemed to be talking at once.

Dulcie smiled politely and said 'Hi' at each introduction, feeling rather dazed, and when there wasn't anyone left to be introduced to, she sat back and sipped her drink, her gaze flitting around the room.

Snippets of conversation reached her ears, but she couldn't follow any of them so she let it flow over her, just happy at the prospect of making new friends. She knew it was going to take time to fit in, but it was something she would have to put some effort into if she wanted to make a new life for herself in Picklewick.

After about half an hour or so she began to relax, and although she still felt like a newbie, people were very kind, going out of their way to talk to her and include her in the conversation. She was particularly drawn to Charity, who was only a couple of years younger than her, and although Dulcie got the impression the girl was quite shy, she was very friendly and had a dry sense of humour. Dulcie was a little concerned when Charity suggested that she popped down to the stables for a riding lesson, but hopefully a love of horses wasn't a prerequisite for a growing friendship, because Dulcie had no intention of going anywhere near a horse.

Dulcie was halfway through telling Megan, an older lady who owned a cake decorating business, about her run-in with Walter's tame sheep, when a familiar voice made her ears prick up. Swivelling around in her chair, she spotted Otto and Walter at the bar.

Hastily she turned back, a blush creeping into her cheeks. For some reason she hadn't expected to see Otto in The Black

Horse this evening, although this was his local too, and the sight of him unsettled her. Her heart did that trippety-trip thing again, and her stomach seemed to tie itself in knots. She licked her lips nervously and took a gulp of her drink, spluttering when it went down the wrong way.

By the time she had finished coughing, people had shuffled around to make way for Otto and Walter to pull up a chair. Otto was now seated next to her, with Petra on her left.

Walter was next to Amos, and the two old gents immediately fell into conversation, leaving Otto to say hello on both their behalf.

Dulcie was watching him carefully as he made his way around everyone, and when he came to her his eyes widened for a second as he noticed her studying him.

'I didn't expect to see you here,' he said, leaving Dulcie to ponder whether he was wishing she wasn't.

'Petra invited me.'

He smiled politely, his gaze glancing around the room before coming back to rest on her. He looked uncomfortable, and she wondered why, hoping it had nothing to do with her.

But why should it? She was reading too much into things, second guessing herself as she so often did, and she could almost hear her mother say, "the world doesn't revolve around you, you know."

'Nice to see you,' Petra said to Otto. 'We were beginning to think you'd turned into a hermit.'

'Dad fancied a pint,' Otto said, making Dulcie think that if his dad hadn't, Otto would have been quite happy to have stayed at home.

'How are you settling into the cottage?' Petra's husband asked.

'It's okay.' Otto shot Walter a look and his expression relaxed when he saw that his father wasn't taking any notice of the conversation. 'It's not been easy,' he admitted, lowering his voice. 'For either of us.'

'Your dad looks better than the last time I saw him,' Petra observed. 'Not so frail. It must be all that good food you're feeding him.'

'I don't know about that,' Otto chuckled. 'He keeps complaining that it's too fancy – although he was happy enough to gobble up a three-course meal last night.'

'**Three** courses!' Petra exclaimed. 'I can tell you're a chef. We're lucky if we get one course and a slice of cake afterwards. What did you have? Not that I would cook it myself, you understand...although Harry is becoming a dab hand in the kitchen.'

'What is it with you women not wanting to cook?' Otto joked. 'Dulcie tells me she doesn't like cooking much either. She doesn't mind eating, though. There wasn't a scrap left.'

Petra raised her eyebrows. 'A scrap of what?' She looked from Otto to Dulcie, then back again.

Dulcie blushed. 'Otto invited me for dinner at his place last night.'

Petra cocked her head. 'I see.'

'It's not like that,' Dulcie blustered.

'Like what?' Her new friend was grinning broadly.

'Otto was just....' Dulcie didn't feel it was her place to go into details. If Otto wanted to share his recipe book idea, that was up to him. But she hadn't wanted Petra to get the wrong end of the stick and think there was something going on between her and Otto when there wasn't.

'Being friendly?' Petra drawled.

'Exactly!'

Otto, Dulcie noticed, had failed to say anything, and when someone asked Petra a question and her attention was otherwise engaged, Dulcie whispered, 'I hope I didn't speak out of turn?'

'You didn't,' he assured her in an equally quiet voice. 'Although I am grateful you didn't mention my cookbook idea.'

'Eaten any more of the hedgerow recently?' she murmured.

'Not today. Dad was very pleased to have an old-fashioned cottage pie for dinner.'

'It sounds lovely. I had egg on toast.'

'Oh, dear...You could have eaten with us if I'd—'

'God, sorry! I wasn't angling for an invite— Honest!' Dulcie could feel her already warm cheeks burst into flame.

Amusement shone in his eyes. 'I didn't think you were. But I've got a habit of making too much, and there is loads left over. I could drop a portion up to the farm later, if you like?'

'Please don't trouble yourself.'

'It isn't any trouble, honestly. In fact, why don't you stop off on the way home, and pick it up?'

'I didn't drive – Petra brought me in her car.'

'How about if I take you back later? I'm sure Petra won't mind.'

Petra heard her name being mentioned and asked, 'What won't I mind?'

'If I drive Dulcie home,' Otto said.

Dulcie caught her eye. Petra was grinning at her again.

'I don't mind at all,' the woman chortled.

'Excuse me, I'll be back in a sec,' Dulcie said, getting to her feet and grabbing her bag. She didn't need to go to the loo, but it was a good excuse to be on her own for a few minutes to calm her furiously beating heart.

But when she got there, all the cubicles were taken. Dithering about whether to wait, she settled for washing her hands and redoing her lipstick.

'I never thought we'd see Otto York in Picklewick,' a voice from one of the cubicles said, and for a second Dulcie thought the comment was aimed at her, until another voice piped up.

'Neither did I. Do you think he's got a girlfriend?'

'Why? Are you volunteering for the position?' the first woman asked.

'I wouldn't mind trying. He's a bit of a dish. Did you see the way he was looking at that woman sitting next to him? Like he wanted to eat her up? Do you think they're together?'

'I don't believe so. She arrived with Petra.'

'Huh! It's a wonder **she's** not after him herself.'

'Sour grapes, Cher. Just because Harry was interested in her and not you.'

One of the toilets flushed, then the other.

Not wanting to be caught eavesdropping, Dulcie beat a hasty retreat, her ears burning. What was all that about? *Had* Otto been looking at her in that way?

She wasn't ready to return to the others just yet, and she definitely wasn't ready to face Otto, so to give herself some breathing space she headed outside to the beer garden.

There was no escaping him, though.

Otto was already out there, a drink in his hand and a thoughtful expression on his face.

But if she hoped she could slip back inside without him noticing her, she was sorely mistaken. He clapped eyes on her as soon as she stepped outside, and unless she wanted to be rude, she had no choice other than to keep going as he beckoned her over.

'Too much?' he asked, as she slid onto the bench opposite.

'A bit,' she admitted. 'Everyone seems to know everyone else.'

'That's Picklewick for you.'

'Hi, Otto.'

Dulcie and Otto looked up. Dulcie recognised the voice as belonging to Cher, one of the women in the ladies' toilets, and her heart sank

The woman was gorgeous, as Dulcie's quick head-to-toe scan showed. Glossy dark hair bounced on her shoulders, her make-up was skilfully not-there, she had long deep-red nails, and her clothes looked as though she had just stepped off a catwalk.

Dulcie had an immediate attack of envy. No matter how hard she tried, she would never be able to achieve Cher's level of chic sophistication.

'Uh, hi. Do I know you?' Otto asked politely.

'No, but don't let that stop us from being friends.' The woman simpered, and Dulcie scowled. 'I'm Cher. I heard you were living in Picklewick. Are you putting down roots here, or is this a pit stop?'

'I'm from here, actually,' he said.

'Scoot over.' The woman shoved her bum onto the bench, nearly sitting on his lap in the process.

Otto scooted, but Cher was still too close for Dulcie's liking, although Otto didn't seem to mind that her thigh was touching his. Or that she had placed a proprietary hand on his arm and was gazing at him adoringly.

'I'd best get back to the others,' Dulcie said. 'They'll be wondering where I've got to.'

Otto made to get up, but Cher pulled him back down, saying, 'Tell me, where are you working at the moment? I'd love to book a table and sample your...' she paused suggestively '... food.'

The woman was a man-eater. Dulcie wanted to gag, and as she hurried away Otto's reply faded as she headed inside.

She was tempted to walk straight through the pub and out into the street, but she didn't think it fair to Petra if she disappeared without giving her some explanation. Petra had been kind enough to invite her, and Dulcie didn't want to throw that back in her face.

So she went over to her and whispered in her ear.

'I'll drive you home,' Petra offered, on hearing Dulcie's flimsy excuse that she had a headache.

'Nonsense! You stay and enjoy the evening. I can find my own way back, and the fresh air will do me good.'

'Are you sure?'

'Absolutely. Thank you for inviting me this evening, it was fun. Could you pass on my apologies to the others? I'm sorry to sneak off, but I think it must be all the paint fumes I've inhaled over the past week.'

'Let me give you my mobile number. Text me when you get home. And if I haven't heard from you in an hour, I'll be sending out a search party.'

'Thanks, Petra.' Impulsively Dulcie gave her a peck on the cheek, then slipped quietly away.

'Oi! Otto! Have you got a minute?' Otto saw Petra waving at him from the door to the bar, and relief at the interruption washed over him.

He hadn't wanted to be rude, but he was getting to the point where he was seriously considering telling Cher to back off. Talk about coming on too strong! The woman didn't know the meaning of subtlety.

To be fair, she was exactly the type he was usually attracted to, and maybe she sensed it. In his other life, he would have flirted with her as hard as she was flirting with him, enjoying her confidence and her "I know what I want and I know how to get it" attitude. They would have understood each other – she would have wanted to be with him for his minor celebrity status and the opportunity to be photographed with him, and he would have been happy to spend time with an attractive woman. He wouldn't have taken it seriously, and neither would she: especially when she realised that being a chef was not as glamorous as it appeared. Long hours, hard work and a determination to be the best in the business didn't make good boyfriend material. Which was probably why he was still single at thirty-four. That, and the fact that he had yet to meet anyone he wanted to have more than a few dates with.

Until, that is, he had met Dulcie. But he was pretty sure she didn't think of him in that way, which was a shame.

'Excuse me,' he said to Cher, who was scowling worse than a five-year-old child. 'I had better see what Petra wants.' He got to his feet and Cher's scowl immediately turned into a sexy pout.

'Promise me you'll come back?' she drawled.

'Er, I don't think I'll be able to. I'm with my father, you see.'

'Perhaps we could catch up another time?'

'Perhaps. Nice meeting you,' he said, and made his escape before she could suggest swapping phone numbers. Or, god forbid, try to pin him down to a time and a place.

'Is it my dad?' Otto asked as soon as he reached Petra, a worm of worry uncoiling in his stomach.

'Your dad?' Petra looked puzzled, then her face cleared. 'Your dad is fine. He's reminiscing with Amos. I didn't know Walter had a brother?'

'Uh, yeah, Uncle Emrys. He emigrated to Australia thirty-odd years ago. Died last year. I never met him. What was it you wanted to have a word about?'

Petra blinked. 'Oh, right. It's about Dulcie. She's gone home.'

Otto frowned. 'Why?'

'A headache, she said, but I don't believe her.' Petra looked into the garden and wrinkled her nose when she spotted Cher.

Otto was disappointed; he had been looking forward to spending a couple more hours with Dulcie this evening and he had been hoping to drive her home.

'Why don't you believe her?' he asked, as Petra's words sank in.

'Because she refused a lift. Said she'd walk back.'

'So?'

Petra rolled her eyes, her exasperation evident. 'It's getting dark and Dulcie doesn't strike me as the type of woman who does much walking along lonely country lanes at night.'

'You're right!' Otto could have slapped himself for not realising. 'Why do you think she decided to leave?'

Petra gave him a pointed look and glanced into the garden again, before meeting his gaze. 'Why do you think?' she countered.

'Cher?' He hazarded a guess.

'Give the man a gold star. Oops, I forgot, you already have one,' Petra smirked. 'Seriously, I think someone should go after her, and as she only knows me and you, and I have the baby with me, I think it should be you. If you hurry, you can catch her up. When you find her, there's no need to come back to the pub – I'll drive Walter home.'

Otto gave her a searching look. Was Petra trying to set him up? Had she guessed that he was starting to have feelings for Dulcie?

It didn't matter. The only thing he was concerned about right now was Dulcie's safety.

'Thanks, Petra. Tell Dad I'll see him later,' he said.

He thought he heard Petra mutter, 'Or in the morning,' but he was sure he must have misheard.

Putting it out of his mind, he hurried out of the pub and into the deepening twilight.

Stupidly, Dulcie hadn't expected dusk to be quite so dark.

She had left the village and the comfort of the streetlights behind (which had only just come on) and was now walking along the road leading to Muddypuddle Lane. The problem was, it was getting dark faster than she had anticipated, and the turning into Muddypuddle Lane was further than she thought. The distance seemed much shorter in a car.

And to make matters worse, she had a feeling she was being followed.

Dulcie glanced behind nervously and her stomach churned when she saw a silhouette pass under the last streetlight, heading in her direction.

She pursed her lips and carried on walking.

Although the outskirts of the village were unlit, the road had a couple of houses on it, so whoever it was probably lived in one of those and wasn't following her at all, she reasoned.

But as the last house faded into the distance, she looked over her shoulder to see a dark figure still following her and she began to worry.

Her concern deepened as she realised the person was catching her up, and Dulcie's palms grew clammy and her pulse quickened in fear.

Why had she been so silly? If she had accepted the offer of a lift, she could have been at home by now, making herself a cup of cocoa to cry into. Better still, she should have shoved her jealousy to the back of her mind and concentrated on enjoying the evening and making new friends.

She already knew that a man like Otto was out of her league, and he'd given her no indication that he fancied her, so she shouldn't have felt put out when he had shown an interest in a woman who was more his type.

The scuff of a shoe on tarmac made her flinch.

The pavement had petered out several metres ago, and the road had abruptly become a dangerous and threatening one.

Trying not to be obvious about it, Dulcie shifted her bag to the front and quietly undid the zip. If she could find her keys, she could grip one of them between her knuckles to use as a weapon.

'Dulcie.'

Oh, god, he knew her name. How did he—

'Dulcie! Wait up.'

She drew in a sharp breath, relief making her knees weak as she recognised the voice. Trembling, she slowed to a halt.

Her heart still thumped though, but now it was because of Otto himself, and not because she was frightened of being attacked.

'What are you doing here?' she asked, her voice squeaky with adrenalin.

'Making sure you get home okay. It's getting dark.'

Her eyes widened. Maybe she'd read him wrong and he was interested after all, and she was inordinately pleased that he hadn't stayed in the pub with Cher.

'Where's your car?' she asked. Although *Otto* might have walked into Picklewick, she guessed that his dad wouldn't have been up for it, so she guessed he had driven to The Black Horse.

'At the pub. I assumed you would have cut across the fields, and if I'd driven I would have missed you.'

'Why would I cut across the fields?'

'Because it's quicker. There's a public footpath leading from the edge of the village, past the stables, and up onto the hillside.'

'I didn't realise.' But Dulcie was fairly certain that she wouldn't have taken it, even if she had known about it.

'Remind me to show you,' he said, falling into step beside her. 'How are you feeling?'

'Eh?'

'Your headache?'

'Er, better thanks. Fresh air helped.' She hoped he couldn't hear the fib in her voice. If it had been light enough to see her face, he definitely would have realised she wasn't telling the truth, because she'd never been good at lying.

They walked in companionable silence for a while before Otto said, 'I hope you weren't too intimidated.' And for a second, Dulcie thought he was referring to Cher, before he added, 'Not like I was. I hardly knew a soul there. The only person I know is Amos. He and my dad go way back. He's lived at the stables for about forty years.'

Dulcie was surprised. She had assumed Otto was friends with everyone at their table this evening.

He continued, 'I was already in college by the time Petra moved in with Amos, so although I've bumped into her over the years, I can't say I really know her.'

'She seems nice,' Dulcie said. It was strange to think that even though Otto had grown up on Lilac Tree Farm, he was almost as much a stranger here as she.

'Yes, she is,' Otto agreed. 'She was the one who told me you'd gone home, and suggested I come after you.'

'Oh. I see.' Dulcie felt disheartened. It hadn't been his idea after all. It had been Petra's. He had probably felt obliged.

She didn't say anything more, pretending to have to save her breath for the hike up the hill. Muddypuddle Lane was quite steep when you had to walk up it from the bottom, she realised. It was bad enough plodding up it from Otto's cottage. Coming from the bottom was quite a trek and Dulcie was puffing by the time they reached the entrance to the farmyard.

She fully expected Otto to say goodnight to her at this point, and was surprised when he escorted her right to her door.

'Thanks,' she said. 'I'm glad Petra made you come after me. It's twice as long on foot as it is by car and I didn't realise how scary it would be.'

'She didn't **make** me. I would have followed you anyway.'

He would have? She inhaled slowly, hoping the reason was that he liked her and not just because he was a considerate guy.

Otto hesitated and she wondered what he was going to say, but he didn't say anything. Instead, what he did next thrilled, shocked, and excited her in equal measure.

He *kissed* her.

His lips were soft and warm, and for the briefest of moments she froze. Then she was kissing him back with an ardour she hadn't felt in a very long time. If ever...

Her mouth opened and his tongue slipped inside. His arms wrapped around her, his embrace tight and urgent, and she was swept away by the passion he evoked, until she was breathless and dizzy. Every nerve ending burned and sizzled, until she thought she might burst into flames.

When they eventually broke apart, she was left with trembling knees, a racing pulse, and a surge of desire so strong that it was all she could do not to drag him inside and take him to bed.

He still held her, and she could feel the tension in his arms and hear his ragged breathing, and she knew he wanted her as much as she wanted him.

His voice was hoarse when he spoke. 'I'm so glad it was you who won the farm.'

'So am I,' she murmured. Then she let out a nervous giggle as she added raggedly,

'If the new owner had been a man, I couldn't imagine you kissing **him**.'

'I've been imagining kissing you since the day we met.'

The words blazed a path through her mind, and her heart soared.

'You can do it again if you like,' she suggested, thinking **please do it again**, before asking, 'Do you want to come in?' knowing full well what it would lead to if he did. And from the hunger in his eyes, she didn't think he'd refuse.

He smiled, a slow seductive upturn of his lips that made her tummy tighten in anticipation, turning her into a pool of liquid heat. His growl of, 'Hell, yes,' made her quiver, desire swamping her until all she could think of was this gorgeous, delectable man.

Her heart thudding, Dulcie unlocked the door and pushed it open. 'Do you want a coffee?' she asked in an attempt to slow things down.

But it was a futile gesture.

'I want *you*,' he said, and she drew in a sharp breath.

He inched closer and she leant towards him, the lift of her chin and the tilt of her head an unmistakable invitation, as anticipation sent every cell of her body into overdrive.

Suddenly she was in his arms, and he was holding her so tightly and kissing her so thoroughly that she couldn't breathe. Her head swam and her legs trembled as she kissed him back, her tongue slipping into his mouth. His groan of desire fuelled her own hunger, and her arms wrapped around his neck as their bodies pressed together.

She felt his firm fingers digging into her hair, and he deepened the kiss until all she could think about was his lips, his tongue, his hand cupping her breast, and the fire he had ignited.

She would have made love to him then and there, in her hall, but he dragged his mouth away and she almost sobbed in frustration as his eyes found hers and he gazed into her soul, stripping her bare.

Whatever he was searching for, he seemed to find it. Then his lips were on hers once more, and she forgot who she was and where she was, for a very long time indeed.

'Did you get much sleep?' Otto asked as Dulcie stirred and opened her eyes. He was propped on his elbow, the sheet around his waist, their legs entwined.

'A little,' she said, her cheeks blooming as she recalled the reason why she had only managed a couple of hours. And how wonderful and magical it had been. This morning she felt both energised and delightfully languid. Her whole body felt as though it had turned to liquid, each limb loose and heavy.

She had never felt so relaxed.

But as he continued to gaze at her, her body began to spark into life once more, and when his lips curled into a slow, seductive smile, every synapse tingled and fizzed with renewed longing.

Dear god, she couldn't get enough of this man. Nor he her, to her delight and surprise.

But finally, they were sated, and Dulcie felt the lure of tea and toast. All that exercise had made her hungry.

Kissing him on the shoulder, she slipped out from underneath his arm and reached for her onesie.

'How am I supposed to get at you when you're wearing that?' he asked, a playful frown furrowing his brow.

'I'm sure you'll find a way,' she said primly. 'But not yet. I'm starving.'

'Now you come to mention it, I could probably do with something to eat.' He rolled out of bed, allowing her a glimpse of his perfect behind and slim hips.

Oh, my...

Giving herself a mental shake – not only was she hungry but the chickens needed to be let out of the henhouse – she promised herself she would drag him back to bed after breakfast. Maybe they could share a shower?

Her pulse leapt at the thought, but she told herself to behave. Food first, love later. Not too much later though, she hoped.

Leaving him to get dressed, Dulcie went downstairs to put the kettle on. Whilst it was coming to the boil, she dashed outside to let the chickens out, scattering some poultry feed on the ground as she did so, smiling at the flurry of feathers and squawks as the three hens squabbled over their breakfast.

Otto was in the kitchen when she returned. He was fully dressed, much to her dismay, and he was also wearing his shoes.

'Tea and toast?' she asked.

'I'd prefer coffee, if you've got it. But if not, tea is fine. Then I'd better go check on my dad,' he said.

'Oh. Okay.' She busied herself by popping some bread in the toaster, so he wouldn't see how disappointed she was. 'I've only got coffee bags. I expect you're used to grinding your own beans and stuff.'

He laughed. 'I'll have you know that I'm quite partial to a coffee bag. So much more convenient.'

'Milk and sugar?'

'Black, please.'

Of course he takes it black, she thought –
he looks like a black-coffee kind of guy.
She realised how little she knew about
him, and how exciting it was going to be
to find out. She couldn't wait!

Taking a couple of mugs off the stand,
she sneaked glances at him out of the
corner of her eye.

Never mind his cooking, Otto himself
looked good enough to eat this morning.

His hair was tousled where she had
repeatedly run her fingers through it, he
had a shadow of stubble covering his jaw,
and as he leant against the doorway his
eyes smouldered when he caught her
staring.

His pupils grew large and his lips parted,
and with a soft growl he opened his arms.

'Dad can wait a while longer. Come here.'

Dulcie was more than happy to oblige.

CHAPTER EIGHT

'Well, well, well,' his dad drawled as Otto sheepishly slipped into the house sometime later. 'I don't need to ask where you spent the night.'

Heat crept into Ottos' cheeks. 'I like her.'

'I should hope so!'

'A lot,' Otto added, for good measure.

'Enough to keep you in Picklewick?'

Otto turned shocked eyes on his father. 'I've no intention of going anywhere.'

'Because of me?' Walter asked. 'And what happens when I'm fighting fit again? Will you go back to London?'

'I don't know.'

'You don't think I'm able to take care of myself, do you?'

Otto decided to be truthful. 'No, Dad; you're getting better, but you're not quite there yet.'

'But I'll get there, son. I'll get there.'

Otto wasn't sure whether the words were a promise or a warning. He also wasn't sure whether he would ever be able to go back to London and leave his elderly father to cope on his own again. Otto was under no illusion that a return to the city would mean a return to his former frantic way of life, with little time to pop back to Muddypuddle Lane to check on his dad.

No, he had to accept that his home was in Picklewick for the foreseeable future, and that he should concentrate on writing his book.

To be honest, he was looking forward to this new challenge in his life. If Dulcie, who by her own admission was no foodie, loved the dishes he had prepared for her the other night, then other people surely would. He had done his research and knew that there were plenty of books on cooking foraged ingredients already on the market, but he was hoping his would be easily accessible to everyone, no matter how poor a cook they believed themselves to be. And with that in mind, he vowed to try to persuade Dulcie to have a go at cooking one of his recipes –

even if it was as basic as picking fresh clover from her garden and mixing it up with salad leaves and a tangy fresh dressing.

Otto had a quick shower, then made some breakfast (although according to his dad, it was more like brunch) then he got to work on preparing Sunday lunch: roast beef with all the trimmings.

Should he ask Dulcie to join them?

He wanted to, and not just because he guessed she probably wouldn't be cooking a proper meal for herself. It had only been a couple of hours since he'd kissed her goodbye, but he already longed to see her again.

As he swiftly sliced carrots into batons, he chuckled wryly. Who would have guessed that he would become besotted with the new owner of Lilac Tree Farm? And besotted was definitely the right word. He hadn't been able to stop thinking about her since the very first time they'd met, and last night had compounded the problem. Every time he blinked, her image flashed across his inner eye, and he could still feel the softness of her in his arms, taste her lips, smell her vanilla-scented skin...

In all his thirty-four years he had never experienced such a thing. No woman had touched him as deeply as Dulcie, and it was rather worrying. What if she didn't feel the same way? What if last night hadn't meant as much to her as it had to him?

The stupid thing was, he had known her for less than a week!

Take it slow, he cautioned.

Although...having spent the night with her, he did wonder if it was far too late for that kind of advice.

The last thing Dulcie felt like doing today was picking up a paintbrush, but she couldn't sit around all day mooning over Otto, and she had to do something to take her mind off the events of last night – and this morning. He had finally left after another energetic session of lovemaking, and she had watched him jog down the lane, feeling silly that she was missing him already.

The house felt empty without him; so much so that she even tried to tempt Puss inside to keep her company. She could see the ginger tom lying in the planter, basking in the sun, but when she opened a pouch of cat food and called him, all he did was stretch, yawn and turn his back on her, waving his tail in the air to give her a look at his backside as he sauntered off.

As she prised open a tin of white gloss and gave the pot a stir, she decided it wouldn't do her any good to think about Otto all day. And neither did she want to think about work: tomorrow was Monday, her first day in work since she had taken possession of the farm. So she resorted to what had rapidly become a favourite pastime – imagining what could be done with the farm if only she had the funds.

Structurally, she would leave the sitting room as it was, because it was a lovely-sized square room and the fireplace was to die for, although it was in dire need of a new ceiling (Artex? ugh) and she would like to replace the carpet. New curtains wouldn't go amiss either, and neither would new furniture.

The dining room was a different proposition, though. She was currently using it as an office, but in an ideal world she would like to separate her living space from her working space and install an office in one of the outbuildings – the large stone shed with lots of rooms would be perfect. One of those would make an excellent office. Mind you, she wasn't sure how much longer she wanted to stay in her current job, and she was dreading starting back to work tomorrow, so if she found another which didn't require her to work from home, she mightn't have need of an office at all.

Anyway, back to the house itself – which was a much more pleasurable thing to think about even if she didn't have the funds to do much of what she wanted to do. One of those things involved a major expense, because she would dearly love to knock down the wall between the kitchen and the dining room, to make it into one large space. She would have an island where the wall used to be, and a huge window at the front to let in lots of light, as well as to make the most of that fabulous view.

Then she snorted. Who was she kidding? She could barely afford the paint and wallpaper she had bought, let alone plan any major structural work. Anyway, before she did all that, she desperately needed a new bathroom.

Dulcie picked up the tin of paint, then put it back down again as a feeling of defeat swept over her. All this decorating was akin to sticking a plaster on a broken leg. She might make it look better on the surface, but the improvement was only marginal.

Maybe she should just sell up and be done with it?

It was a thought...

Instead of resuming her painting, Dulcie made a cup of coffee and took it outside to enjoy the sunshine. And think.

She didn't want to do anything drastic, however she was torn between wanting to stay on the farm, and not wanting the expense or the hassle to make the house into the place she would call her forever home. She simply didn't have the money and probably never would, so perhaps it was better to cut her losses now, before she spent any more on it.

Walter and Otto mightn't have been able to sell the farm, but that was because it had been laden down with debt. She had no such restriction. However, any money she got for the sale would be hers and hers alone, to do with as she wished. She could use the proceeds to buy a house in the village, somewhere that didn't need a vast amount spent on it, somewhere she could happily invite her family to visit and not worry that they would think she had won a pig in a poke.

She would be sorry to leave the farm though, because she could see its potential, and she still hadn't fully let go of her dreams of wandering barefoot through the meadow or picking apples straight from the tree.

If only there was some way of raising money—

Dulcie gasped as a thought struck her. Maybe there was!

Abandoning her half-drunk coffee, she hurried inside. She had some research to do!

'Can I ask you a favour?' Otto said, a week or so later. He nuzzled Dulcie's neck, making her squirm in delight.

'It depends,' she replied, warily.

'Will you try out a recipe for me?'

'You know I will! You can cook for me anytime.' She wriggled around to kiss him properly, moving one of the cushions out of the way. They were snuggled together on the sofa in the living room of the farmhouse, supposedly watching a film, but there was far more kissing going on than watching tv.

It was all very domesticated and quite lovely. In fact, the whole week had been quite lovely, with Otto popping up to the farm in the evenings, often – but not always – spending the night. He sometimes brought food with him, and other times he would cook for her. She would watch him potter around in her kitchen and wonder if he found it strange. After all, he had taught himself to cook in it when he was a boy and here he was cooking in it again; however, it didn't belong to his dad anymore – it belonged to her – and according to Otto it hadn't altered much over the years either, which probably made it even more of an odd experience for him.

Hopefully, if her plans came to fruition, that might change when the kitchen and dining room became one large spacious room, with a state-of-the-art kitchen for him to enjoy.

It wouldn't be just for Otto, of course, because who knew if their relationship would last. It was still very early days and although they couldn't keep their hand off each other, the L-word hadn't been mentioned yet. Dulcie was falling for him badly, but she wasn't sure he felt the same. She hoped he did, but...

'That's not quite what I meant,' he said, chuckling. 'I want **you** to cook for **me.**'

Dulcie laughed disbelievingly. 'Will beans on toast do you?'

'I'm serious. I want to check whether someone who doesn't like to cook can actually follow one of my recipes and make a decent job of it. I'm hoping my dishes will be easy enough for everyone.'

'You're serious?'

He nodded, his expression pleading. 'Please?'

Dulcie narrowed her eyes and gazed at him slyly. 'You'll have to ask me very nicely.'

'How nicely?' His lips fluttered against the side of her mouth. 'As nicely as this?'

'I'm sure you can do better.'

He trailed kisses down her neck. 'How about this?'

'Hmm...'

'This?' His lips had reached her collarbone, but by then speech was beyond her, and it was some considerable time before she was able to utter anything coherent.

Otto watched Dulcie chopping a couple of shallots and itched to take over, worried that she was about to slice a finger off.

He held back though, because this was supposed to be about a reluctant cook attempting one of his recipes, so he concentrated on making notes instead and tried not to interfere.

'What's the difference between shallots and onions?' she asked, her tongue poking out a little as she concentrated. 'Can't I use onions instead?'

'You could, but shallots are sweeter and have more flavour. Do you think I should mention in the recipe that shallots can be swapped for onions?'

'Yes. I wasn't quite sure what shallots were and it might have put me off.'

Otto wasn't convinced, but he was willing to take her advice on board, although he was fairly certain that people who knew what chickweed was, would probably be familiar with shallots.

'Done,' she announced, putting the knife down. 'Now what?'

Otto bit back a smile. 'Read the recipe.'

'It says to melt a knob of butter in a pan and fry the shallots gently for a couple of minutes. Then add the potato and fry for another five minutes.'

'Okay, then, that's what you need to do.'

'How much is a knob?' she wanted to know.

'About forty grammes.'

'I think you should say that. A knob could mean anything.'

'Agreed.' Otto made a note. See, this was why he needed a non-chef to cook the dishes he was creating. After years of practise, he instinctively knew how much butter was needed, but most people might appreciate a bit of guidance.

The aroma of frying shallots filled the kitchen and he inhaled deeply, enjoying the familiar smell. He'd make a decent cook out of Dulcie yet, he vowed.

'I've got to add the vegetable stock next and simmer for ten minutes,' she read, pouring the stock out of a jug and into the pan. As soon as she had finished, she turned to him and asked, 'Can I have a kiss now?'

'Not until we're done,' Otto protested. 'You know it won't stop at one kiss.'

Dulcie pouted and he fought the urge to gather her into his arms and whisk her off to bed.

He settled for drinking her in, instead.

The first time he had seen her he'd thought she was gorgeous, and time had only served to strengthen his initial impression. She was more than gorgeous – she was delectable. Sweet, funny, kind, playful, oddly naive in some ways...she was perfect, inside and out. Aside from being unable to keep his hands off her, Otto was also unable to keep his gaze off her. His dad had accused him of looking like a love-sick puppy whenever Dulcie was around, but he couldn't help himself.

Anyway, his dad was just as enamoured. Walter thought the world of her already, and had told him on more than one occasion that he was chuffed to bits that Otto and Dulcie were an item.

Otto was pretty chuffed too.

Dulcie's face fell when she opened the email from Prodine Estates – it wasn't the news she had been hoping for, and not only that, they had also taken their own sweet time in getting back to her. But now that they had, she was flummoxed.

She had sent the estate agent an email a couple of weeks ago, asking whether they would be interested in selling a field or three for her. She had scoured the internet for hours, trying to discover what the selling price of agricultural land was in the area, but she hadn't had a great deal of luck as there were so many variables. But she reasoned that anything she got for her fields was better than nothing, and she could put the money towards renovations on the house. After all, she was hardly going to farm them herself, was she? She still disliked sheep, and she couldn't see that changing any time soon.

But this email had suggested something else entirely, and she read it again, this time aloud and more carefully.

'Blah...blah...thank you for contacting us...blah...blah.'

She paused, having come to the bit that had thrown her into a tizzy. 'After careful consideration we would be interested in securing Lilac Tree Farm ourselves and in its entirety,' she recited. 'We are aware that planning permission has been granted for the conversion of existing outbuildings on a property nearby, and we are confident that this may well be the case for conversion of your outbuildings into sympathetic dwellings. Of course, planning permission would have to be sought and granted before any sale were to take place, and with this in mind we would politely request that you make an appointment with one of our agents to visit your property for an initial and without prejudice discussion.'

Dulcie blew out her cheeks. Blimey! She hadn't been expecting that.

She was aware that Petra had converted an old cow shed into three holiday cottages, and that Amos was currently in the process of transforming a feed store into a bungalow for him and Lena, his lady friend, to live in.

But what Dulcie hadn't been aware of was the possibility that her own outbuildings might also have a new lease of life as private homes. And she certainly hadn't anticipated that Prodine Estates might want to buy the whole lot themselves – the farmhouse included.

Which meant that she would have to look for somewhere else in Picklewick to live.

But hadn't that same thought already crossed her mind, and hadn't she dismissed it because she really did like living in the farmhouse, especially since it was only a short walk from Muddypuddle Cottage and Otto?

It wouldn't hurt to speak with them though, would it? And she might be pleasantly surprised. She had no real idea what the farm was worth, but as she had previously told herself, anything she got from selling it would be pure profit – profit which she could then use to buy a nice little cottage.

No, it most definitely wouldn't hurt to speak to them.

'It's our one-month anniversary soon,' Otto had said yesterday. 'I think we should celebrate.'

Dulcie's eyes lit up and she had given him a great big grin. How romantic! 'What did you have in mind?' she'd asked, delighted that he'd remembered. Not many men would.

'I thought it might be nice for you to taste someone else's cooking for a change. How about we go to The Falcon for a meal? It's not too far and I hear it's good.'

'Sounds lovely,' she'd replied, and so that was where they were heading now.

Dulcie had dressed up for the occasion and relished the feel of a skirt swirling around her legs and the sight of her painted toenails peeping out of cute sandals. Her dress was light and summery, even though it was only May and still chilly in the evenings. So with that in mind, she had slung a soft leather jacket in a dreamy vanilla colour over her shoulders. She had bought it in the sales a few years ago and it was utterly impractical – which was probably why she adored it so much and didn't wear it very often.

Otto's eyes widened when he saw her, and she wondered whether he was going to sweep her off her feet and take her to bed instead of going out for the promised meal. But he behaved like a perfect gentleman, apart from whispering in her ear that he was looking forward to seeing her without the jacket later, and without the dress...or her underwear.

Dulcie took great satisfaction in telling him that she wasn't wearing any (she was, actually) and seeing his pupils dilate and his eyes darken with hunger.

Giggling, she flounced towards the car, leaving Otto muttering something about her being the death of him.

For a while part of her wished they'd forgone the meal, but she reasoned that they had to eat and she was hungry, so making love could wait for a couple of hours. The anticipation would be exquisite, especially if they carried on flirting the way they were currently doing. She had forgotten how much fun flirting could be, and she was having a great time fluttering her eyelashes at him over the top of the menu, licking her lips suggestively, and once she had even slipped off her sandal and run her foot up and down his leg.

Seeing the strangulated look on his face had her in fits of laughter. But he soon turned the tables on her when he stroked her wrist, leant forward and whispered exactly what he wanted to do to her later.

Dulcie blushed a deeper red than the wine in her glass and had to fan her cheeks with her napkin, which wasn't at all effective, and when the waiter asked if she was alright, she nearly melted into an embarrassed puddle on the floor.

Her discomfort didn't prevent her imagination from going into overdrive though, and she could hardly contain herself all through the meal. For some reason, she sensed that this month-anniversary had marked a milestone for both of them.

Maybe tonight would be the night that he said those three little words?

'I don't think I can move a muscle,' Otto groaned, much later that evening. 'I might just stay in your bed forever.'

'That's fine by me.' Dulcie draped a leg over his, enjoying the feel of his hand as he absently ran it up and down her hip. 'But I do expect food at some point in the near future.'

'You can't be hungry after the huge meal you've just eaten.'

'That was at least two hours ago,' she retorted. 'More like three. Anyway, I was referring to breakfast. I hoped we could have pancakes?' She lifted her head off his shoulder and gave him a winning smile.

'You only want me because I can cook,' he complained.

'That's not true! I want you for your body, too.' She ran her fingers through the smattering of hair on his chest.

'You'll have to wait a while. I'm exhausted.'

'No stamina, that's your problem,' she teased.

'You've worn me out.' He lay there for a moment staring at the ceiling and she wondered if he might be psyching himself up to tell her that he loved her. But she quickly deflated when he said, 'Do you know you've got a crack in the ceiling? Has it been there long?'

'Erm, not that I've noticed.' She blew out her cheeks, and hoped that the roof didn't cave in on them. She could do without this, but it strengthened her resolve to speak with the estate agents. She had an appointment with them on Monday after she'd finished work for the day. 'Oh well, hopefully it won't be my problem for much longer.'

Otto tensed. 'Why is that?' he asked, after a pause which lasted a heartbeat longer than it should have done.

'I've got someone from Prodine Estates coming to see me on Monday.'

Gently Otto extricated his arm from underneath her and sat up. She couldn't see his face properly, but from the tension in his shoulders she didn't think he was pleased.

'What?' she asked, guessing the news had upset him. It was to be expected, but he must understand that she had to do something drastic – the farm was a money-pit. If she did need a new ceiling, she didn't have the money to pay for it. And what if the problem was worse? What if she needed a new *roof*?

Slowly Otto turned to face her and she flinched.

He was staring at her with a shocked expression, which slowly darkened as she watched. His jaw hardened, his mouth narrowed into a line and his eyes grew flinty.

'What's wrong?' she repeated, dread seeping into her bones.

'You want to sell the farm to a **property developer?'** he spat out the last two words.

'Yeah...maybe...I'm not sure. I was only planning on selling a couple of fields, but they're talking about buying the whole lot.' Dulcie stared at him, and her heart plummeted. He looked seriously annoyed. And disappointed.

'You know what they'll want to do, don't you?' he snapped. 'They've got a reputation for building fast and building cheap, and they'll want to cram in as many houses as possible. They'll turn the farm into a bloody housing estate.'

'I know you're upset, but look at it from my point of view. I can't afford to keep the farm going. Not on my wages. It'll bleed me dry before too long.'

'Perhaps you should have thought about that before you bought a ticket.' He flung the duvet back, swung his feet out of bed and hunted around for his clothes.

Dulcie was stunned. She should have anticipated that he would be upset and maybe it was naïve of her not to, but his reaction was way over the top. Besides, he was being naïve too, to assume that the farm would remain the same forever.

Surely he realised that whoever won it would want to do their own thing with it – which might involve selling it.

Perhaps he was right and Prodine Estates did want to build a load of houses on her land, but that was *her* business, not his. It was certainly a question she would be asking them on Monday. Because if that was the case, and they didn't want to renovate the farmhouse and the outbuildings, but wanted to knock them down and build a housing estate there instead, she needed to know.

Fully dressed now, Otto moved towards the door. His face was white, his eyes dark and glittering.

She couldn't believe he was going to walk out on her over this. 'Can we at least talk about it?' she asked.

He hesitated, and for a second she hoped he was going to stay, but instead he said, 'You don't have the slightest interest in rural life, farming, or the village. Picklewick doesn't need characterless boxes – it needs people who respect the land and those who live on it. Over my dead body will you sell even an inch of Lilac Tree Farm to a bloody property developer.'

Shock slammed into her, and her distress turned to anger as his words sunk in. How dare he come over all high and mighty, and try to tell her what she could or couldn't do with her own property.

She hitched in a faltering breath and let it out in a rush. 'So says the man who couldn't wait to leave as soon as he got the chance. You didn't care about it either. You left your poor dad to cope on his own and look how that turned out. Get out.'

'Don't worry, I'm going. And if I so much as hear a whisper about any houses being built on Lilac Tree Farm, so help me I'll…'

She had no idea what it was that he would do, because he whirled on his heel and stormed out before he could tell her.

'Good riddance!' she yelled after him, the front door slamming hard enough to make the house rattle.

Then she promptly burst into tears.

Otto wished he hadn't slammed the door, but he had been so mad that he'd yanked it shut after him as he'd marched through it and hadn't realised his own strength.

He heard Dulcie shout something, but it was lost to the bang of the door and the furious pounding in his ears.

To think he had been about to tell her he loved her!

He could kick himself, he thought, as he stomped across the yard. Dulcie was just like every other woman he had dated. They were only ever concerned about money. Although to be fair, some of them had also quite liked the prestige of being on his arm – until his dad had collapsed and he'd had to come back to the farm to live. After that none of them had wanted to know. Not a single one.

He had hoped Dulcie was different.

Trust him to have fallen in love with her. What an idiot. Despite being intensely attracted to her, he should have had enough sense and self-control, and he also should have realised that a romantic liaison with the person living in what had once been his family home wouldn't work.

She had made it abundantly clear that the farm was hers to do with as she wished, but the thought of houses being built on his fields made his blood boil, despite those fields not belonging to him anymore.

So much for his hope that the new owner of Lilac Tree Farm would actually **farm** the land.

Huh, he must have been wearing rose-tinted glasses.

But he certainly wasn't wearing them now. Dulcie had ripped them off and had trampled all over them. Just like she had trampled over his heart.

Because she owned that just as completely as she owned the farm. And he didn't know how he would be able to live without her.

CHAPTER NINE

One month, that was how long Otto had taken to wreck her life, Dulcie thought, as she sat down at the dining room table on Monday morning and reluctantly opened her laptop.

She wished she could turn the clock back to the moment just before she had bought that damned lottery ticket. If she had known then what she knew now, she would never have bought it. Trust her to enter a gazillion competitions and never win anything – but then when she did finally win something which she thought would be the greatest prize of her life, it had turned out to be a damned booby prize.

With a heavy heart she popped her headphones on and logged in.

She was seriously not in the mood for work today. The only thing she wanted to do was to crawl back into bed, burrow under the covers and pretend the world didn't exist.

Actually, it wasn't the world that was the problem. It was Otto, and her stupid feelings for him. Why did she have to fall in love?

And now he'd gone and spoilt everything.

The farm belonged to her now, and it was up to her what she did with it. If she wanted to sell it – because, let's face it,

what else was she going to do with it? –
it was none of his business.

But he had made it his business, and now
they were over.

He obviously hadn't cared about her that
much, or he wouldn't have flown off the
handle like that. And what he said had
been hurtful. It was unfair of him to
accuse her of not having the slightest
interest in rural life or farming, because
how could she have? She had always
lived in a city and had never experienced
anything like this before, unless a week's
camping holiday on a farm in Devon when
she was ten counted. This was so very
new to her.

Anyway, as she'd said to him, he was a
fine one to talk. He had fled Picklewick
and the farm the very first chance he
could, so who was he to tell her that she

had no interest in the farm, when he hadn't either? Just because he had been forced to return to Muddypuddle Lane, there was no need to take it out on her. Maybe if he had realised sooner that his dad was struggling financially, Otto would have considered selling a field or two himself to get him out of the mess.

Damn him for his double standards and for being so unfair and unreasonable.

With a despondent sigh, Dulcie turned her attention to her job. There would be plenty of time to nurse her broken heart after her shift ended. And she had no doubt that it was broken, because she had completely and utterly fallen in love with him.

How was she supposed to recover from that?

Otto had spent the weekend alternating between seething anger and despair.

The anger was aimed at both Dulcie and himself: Dulcie for not caring about the farm or Picklewick, and himself because he cared too much.

His anger was also salted with a heavy dose of guilt. She was right: he should have come home more often; he should have realised that his father was struggling; he should have played a more active role in the farm – although how he thought he would have been able to do that whilst he was living in London, he didn't know. Mostly though, he felt guilty for being so selfish. If he hadn't left to chase his dreams, his dad wouldn't have lost the farm. And now it belonged to a woman who didn't want to work the land

and who didn't care that years of tradition would be lost when she sold it.

Damn it! What had he been expecting when he'd convinced his dad that the only way to get out of his financial predicament was to get rid of the farm? His foolish hope that it would be won by someone who wanted to run a farm had been exactly that – **foolish.**

But the truth was, he hadn't thought past paying off the farm's debts. He had been far more concerned about his dad's health, both physical and mental, and he still was.

The only good thing to come out of this whole sorry mess was that now that the terrible strain his dad had been under had lifted, his father's health was slowly improving.

For a while Otto thought he was going to lose him, and although his dad wasn't yet at the point where Otto could think about returning to London to try to pick up the pieces of his career, he was beginning to hope that he might be able to do so in the future.

In the meantime, he would be forced to remain in the cottage on Muddypuddle Lane, within a stone's throw of the farm.

Which brought him to the other emotion at the forefront of his mind. His despair was fuelled by the bleak knowledge that for the first time in his life, he was in love. He had even considered telling Dulcie that last night, but thank goodness he hadn't.

'I see your mood isn't any better,' his dad said when he wandered into the kitchen and caught Otto banging pots and pans around, as he prepared to make another foraged-food dish.

This one was dandelion tart, and so far it wasn't going well. He'd not burned garlic since he was in college, and he was cross at his lack of concentration.

'I'm not in a mood,' Otto growled, scowling at the pan.

'Could have fooled me. You're like a bear with a sore head. I haven't said anything until now because I was hoping you would snap out of it, but you're getting worse.'

'I am not.' Otto flung the pan into the sink.

Walter winced at the loud clatter. 'If you behave like this in your own kitchen, I'm surprised you've got any staff left.'

Otto nearly retorted that he didn't have his own kitchen anymore because he didn't have a job, but he bit his lip. His dad felt bad enough as it was, without Otto rubbing it in.

In an effort to lighten the atmosphere and to stop his father from going on about what a bad mood he was supposed to be in, Otto said, 'I thought you realised that all head chefs were prima donnas.'

Walter gave him a disbelieving look. 'You might be a perfectionist, but as far as I know you've never resorted to throwing things. What's up, son? Is it Dulcie?'

'No,' Otto replied shortly, but he could tell from his father's expression that his father wasn't convinced.

'I thought you liked her.' Walter sucked his teeth.

Heat crept into Otto's cheeks, and it wasn't because of the flame from the gas hob. 'I did.' This reply was also short.

'But you don't now?' his dad persisted, and when Otto refused to answer, Walter continued, 'So that's the problem, is it? You like her *too* much.'

Otto's jaw tightened and he pursed his lips.

'I'm right, aren't I?'

'You don't understand.'

'I think I do.' Walter pulled out a chair and dropped into it with a groan. 'You're worried that I'll be upset because you're in love with the woman who owns my farm. Well, I'm not. I've made my peace with the farm having a new owner.'

'No, Dad, you really don't understand. Dulcie is selling Lilac Tree Farm.'

His father sat there for a moment, then rose creakily to his feet and walked slowly out of the kitchen, and Otto watched him go with a concerned expression, but didn't follow him. His dad would deal with the news in his own way and wouldn't appreciate being fussed over.

With a heavy sigh, Otto returned to his cooking, but for once, his heart wasn't in it.

If she had to deal with one more stroppy caller today, Dulcie thought she would scream. Why did people think they could pick up their phone and give her a load of abuse? And didn't they realise that the louder they shouted, the less she was inclined to help them? Of course, she was always professional, and always tried to resolve the situation to the best of her ability.

After a quick comfort break, where she went to the loo, made a cup of coffee (wishing it was something stronger) and took five minutes to calm down, she sat back at the laptop and prepared to do battle once more.

She was in the middle of a call where the customer clearly wasn't right but wasn't prepared to listen to reason (in her experience customers were only right about half of the time) when a volley of bleats from outside was swiftly followed by the door rattling in its frame as a heavy object slammed into it.

Dulcie immediately guessed what it was, and her heart sank.

That damned sheep had got out again and was now trying to butt its way into her house.

'What are you going to do about it, that's what I want to know?' the man on the other end of the phone demanded. His voice had been deep and gruff at first, but it had risen an octave as he'd recounted the problem, and she sensed that his anger had risen along with it.

'I'm sorry, could you repeat that? You cut out for a minute,' she fibbed. She had been distracted by the flippin' sheep and had missed that last bit.

'Don't you give me that nonsense. You heard me the first time. You're just being awkward.'

'I can assure you I'm not, Mr Howes.'

Dulcie winced as Flossie let out a particularly loud bleat. It sounded as though the sheep had made her way to the front of the house and was now directly outside the dining room window.

'Are you making sheep noises?' Mr Howes sounded incredulous. 'You *are*! You're making sheep noises, aren't you?'

'Apologies, Mr Howes, but it's a real sheep—'

'Do you take me for an idiot?'

'Certainly not, I—'

'I want to speak to someone,' he demanded.

 Another bleat. This one was even louder, and rather plaintive.

'I *am* someone, Mr Howes.' It was a pet hate of hers when customers asked to speak to *someone*, as though she was a no one, or a robot.

'Now you're being awkward and patronising, as well as rude. I will not be made fun of, do you hear me?'

Loud and clear, she thought. She would be surprised if *Petra* wasn't able to hear him. She tried again. 'I'm not making fun—'

Damn, her screen informed her that the call had been disconnected and she guessed he had hung up.

Her temper rising, Dulcie yanked the headphones off and slapped them on the table.

'Right,' she muttered grimly, getting to her feet and marching to the door. She might not like sheep, but she was in just the right frame of mind to deal with this one.

'Go away!' she yelled, opening the door. But the words had barely left Dulcie's lips when Flossie shoved her out of the way and barged into the hall, knocking her off her feet.

Landing hard on her backside, the breath whooshed out of her, and when she tried to inhale, she ended up with a faceful of woolly tail as Flossie blundered past, heading for the dining room and the kitchen beyond.

It took Dulcie several minutes of chasing the sheep around the kitchen before she managed to shepherd it out of the back door.

She was hot, even more cross, and utterly exhausted by the time she had cleaned up the little presents the sheep had left for her (yuck!) and finally returned to work. Then she wished she hadn't because the first thing she saw when she looked at the screen was a notification that a customer had made a complaint about her.

So when she heard a knock on the door, she was more than ready to give Otto York a piece of her mind – a really big piece.

'Dad, do you want to be my taster for today?' Otto broke off a morsel of the tart, popped it in his mouth and chewed, before nodding to himself. It tasted fine to him, but it never hurt to get a second opinion, especially one as blunt as his father's.

He reached for a sheet of kitchen towel, broke off another portion of the tart and, holding it carefully, poked his head into the sitting room.

It was empty.

Walter wasn't in his bedroom, and neither was he in the bathroom. The tart cooling rapidly now, Otto peered into the garden.

There was no sign of his father, although Peg was sprawled out on the path, enjoying the morning sunshine.

Maybe he was in the paddock, Otto thought, but Walter was nowhere in sight.

And neither was Flossie, Otto suddenly realised.

'Don't tell me the blasted sheep has escaped again,' he grumbled, and his stomach lurched. The silly old duffer had gone looking for Flossie himself, like some ancient Bo Peep, because he hadn't wanted to bother Otto.

Since Walter had collapsed, sending Otto dashing to the farm, his dad hadn't ventured far. He hadn't been able to.

What if he had a relapse, Otto fretted. He could collapse again, and this time he wouldn't be in his own house and close enough to the phone to call for help. He would be in the lane, or worse – out on the hillside.

Otto dropped the tart on the kitchen counter as he sprinted through the cottage in search of his trainers.

Shoving his feet into them, he grabbed his mobile and his keys, and dashed outside.

There was no sign of his father.

Fairly confident that Flossie would have headed up the lane rather than down it, he began to jog towards the farm, pushing aside the worry that if Flossie hadn't gone 'home' to the farmhouse but had gone in search of her flock mates instead, she could be anywhere.

And so could his father.

It was definitely a member of the York family at her door, Dulcie saw when she opened it. But it wasn't the York she had been expecting to see.

'Walter! Have you come to fetch Flossie? She's out the back, eating the flowers in the garden.'

Dulcie didn't see the point in complaining to him that the stupid animal had forced its way into her house, leaving pellets of poop over her kitchen floor. The poor chap had enough to contend with having Otto for a son. If it had been **Otto** on her step, she would have let him have it with both barrels.

Walter frowned. 'Flossie? I didn't realise she'd got out, sorry. I'll take her with me when I go.' He hesitated. 'Actually, it's you I've come to see.'

'Me?

'What's going on with you and Otto?' He held up a hand before she had a chance to say anything. 'I've asked him, but he won't tell me.'

The elderly gent was breathing heavily and Dulcie noticed that he was clutching the wall for support.

'Come in,' she said, taking his arm and guiding him inside, worried that he might keel over any moment. Otto hadn't gone into detail about his father's health, but for Otto to give up his life in London and come back to Muddypuddle Lane to live, it must have been serious.

'Just for a bit, until I get my breath back,' Walter said. 'You wouldn't happen to have a cup of tea going spare, would you?'

'I would,' she said, eying the laptop as she sidled past it. Work would just have to wait. She grabbed a chair on the way and took it into the kitchen, fearing he might keel over if he didn't sit down soon.

'The kitchen needed a lick of paint,' he said, when he had eased himself into a chair with a grunt. 'It looks all nice and fresh.' His gaze roamed around the old units, before eventually coming to rest on her. 'Well? Are you going to tell me?' he asked.

'I don't think it's my place to,' she replied hesitantly, thinking that if Otto wanted his father to know, he would have told the old man himself.

He shook his head. 'You'll understand when you have kids. All I've ever wanted was for Otto to be happy.' He grunted, 'I've made a right pig's ear of it, dragging him away from London and making him come back to look after an old man.'

'You're not that old.' She popped a couple of tea bags into a pair of mugs.

'Old enough to know better. I'm also old enough to know that my son isn't happy. Lately I thought there was a chance he might be, but these past couple of days...' Walter studied her, his gaze unwavering. 'I might be reading too much into it, but I think you're the reason.'

Dulcie was astounded.

She opened her mouth, hunted unsuccessfully for something to say, then closed it again without uttering a word. Otto had made it pretty clear that he wasn't happy with her, so yes, she *was* the reason he was upset.

But she was upset too.

She had stupidly allowed him to slip into her heart, and when he'd walked out he had left a gaping hole in it that would take time to heal.

Walter continued, 'I might not have spent as much time with my son as I would have liked in recent years, but I know him as well as he knows himself. If I may be so bold, I believe he might be in love with you. And I think you feel the same way about him.'

'We hardly know each other,' Dulcie protested, handing him his tea and nearly scolding herself when she spilt some in shock at what Walter said next.

'That hasn't stopped you from spending every waking minute together for the past few weeks.' His retort was sharp.

When she flinched, his expression softened, and he added, 'All I'm saying is, give love a chance, eh? If it doesn't work out, then so be it.'

'He's mad with me because I said I might be thinking of selling the farm,' she blurted, wringing her hands. 'I'm not a farmer. I don't have the foggiest idea what to do with it. And I need the money. This house isn't cheap to run.'

'Tell me about it,' Walter muttered.

'Sorry.' Dulcie was immediately contrite.

'You won't get much for it,' the old man continued. 'It's hardly prime arable land.'

'I'm hoping Prodine Estates will take it off my hands,' she confessed.

Walter snorted. 'They'll soon lose interest because they won't be able to get planning permission, not for the kind of houses they want to build. But another farmer might be prepared to buy an acre or two for the right price. Or you could keep it. Do something with it yourself...?'

'Like what? I'm not too keen on sheep.'

'Pity. They do well here. As do beef cattle. Dairy, not so much. The grazing is too coarse for them.'

Dulcie shuddered. Cows were even worse than sheep.

'Anyway, I'm sure a bright thing like you will think of something,' Walter said. 'Now, back to you and Otto.'

Before she could say anything, there was another bang on the door, and Dulcie sighed. To think she had imagined that this place would be peaceful. She'd had more interruptions this morning than she used to have in a whole week in her old place.

Expecting it to be the postman, her heart missed a beat when Otto shouted, 'Dulcie? Dulcie!'

'Talk of the devil,' Walter said mildly. He sipped his tea. 'You'd better let him in – he doesn't sound happy.'

With trepidation, she went to open the door.

'Have you seen my dad?' Otto demanded. He looked frantic. 'Flossie got out and I think he's gone looking for her. The daft sod.'

'You'd better come in. He's in the kitchen.'

'Is he alright?' Without waiting for an answer, Otto strode past her, calling, 'Dad? What the hell do you think you're playing at? I've been worried sick.'

Dulcie followed Otto into the kitchen and found him crouching beside his father.

Walter waved him away. 'I'm fine. Stop fussing.'

Otto shook his head in exasperation. He glanced at Dulcie, then back to Walter. 'Dad, if Flossie escapes again, tell me,' he instructed. 'I'll find her.'

'I didn't know she'd got out until I arrived,' Walter said.

'Then why are you—?' Otto stopped. 'Dad!' He looked pained.

Walter took another mouthful of tea, put his mug down and levered himself to his feet. 'I'm going to take Flossie home,' he said. 'Otto, stay here. You and Dulcie need to have a talk. And don't come home until you've sorted things out.'

Dulcie heard the old man calling to the sheep and Flossie's answering bleat, followed by the sound of footsteps and hooves which gradually faded, leaving an uncomfortable silence in their wake.

Neither Dulcie nor Otto said a word for several minutes.

Eventually, Otto broke it. 'I'm sorry, I shouldn't have spoken to you like that.'

'No, you shouldn't have,' Dulcie agreed.

'I wasn't annoyed with you. I was annoyed with myself. It's my fault that Dad lost the farm.'

'You can't blame yourself.'

'But I do. I was selfish.'

'You were doing what was best for you, for your future.'

He pursed his lips. 'As must you. And if that means selling the farm...'

Dulcie let out a small huff. 'You know the proverb 'be careful what you wish for'? Well, I was a competition addict. I entered everything I could in the hope of winning **something**. My ultimate goal was to win enough money on the lottery to buy a house of my own.'

'Instead, you won a farm,' Otto said, his voice loaded with sympathy.

'And I've no idea what to do with it.'

'I do. Let me help you.'

Dulcie gasped. 'So *that* is what this was all about? You've been dating me because of the **farm?**' She could feel anger bubbling to the surface again. The cheek of the man!

'Not even close,' he shot back.

'Then why?' she demanded, her hands on her hips.

'Because I—' Otto inhaled deeply. 'Because I've fallen for you. I really am glad it was you who won the farm – whatever you decide to do with it.

Dulcie studied his face. 'Even if I sell it?'

'Yes.'

'Even though it'll break your heart? This was your home for such a long time—'

'My heart is already broken,' Otto interrupted. 'Because when you sell up you'll move away, and I've got used to you being here.'

'But you're right. I'm not cut out for this lifestyle. I'm not cut out to be a farmer.'

'You don't have to be a farmer. Sell it, if that's what you want. Buy a little place in the village instead.'

'You're serious, aren't you? You honestly don't mind if I sell your family farm?'

'It's not my farm anymore. It's **yours.** And if selling up will make you happy, then so be it. I just pray you'll stay in Picklewick.'

He moved nearer, close enough for her to smell the cologne he wore, and she breathed it in, the scent flooding her senses and making her dizzy.

But she wasn't too dizzy to know that she didn't want to sell the farm. This was part of who Otto was and she knew how much it would hurt him, despite him putting on a brave face. There must be other ways she could raise money... make the farm earn its keep. Just not with sheep. **Definitely** not with sheep.

'I'll stay,' she vowed. She would pick his brains, see what could be done that didn't cost too much, but that was a conversation that could wait for another time, because Otto was saying, 'I realise that a month shouldn't be long enough to fall in love with someone, but I have.'

He pulled a face, a dimple appearing in one cheek, and Dulcie thought how sexy he looked. And sad, too.

'I love you, Dulcie, and I know you don't feel the same way, but could you give me a chance? Give **us** a chance? You never know, in time you might begin to love me.'

'Too late,' she said, and the hope in his eyes flickered out.

He swallowed and looked away, the hurt on his face plain to see.

'It's too late because I've **already** fallen for you,' she clarified.

His gaze snapped to her, and his eyes locked onto hers. What she saw in their depths stole her breath and made her pulse race. Tenderness, love, desire, hope – his emotions mirrored her own.

Her heart soared in response, and she began to tremble with the enormity of it.

As though sensing how she felt, he cupped her face in his hand, his fingers at her temple.

'I've never felt like this before,' she murmured, as his lips slid against hers for a tentative soft kiss.

'Neither have I.' He drew back and gazed into her eyes once more. 'I'm not going to hurt you, and we can take this as fast or as slow as you want.'

'I'm scared,' she confessed.

His laugh was low, rumbling in his chest as he took her in his arms. 'So am I, my love, so am I.'

And suddenly, she wasn't so frightened anymore. This was a new beginning for both of them. A new life lay ahead, and she couldn't wait to start living it.

There are loads more large print books in the Muddypuddle Lane series. Available at all good book stores, or ask your local library.

About Etti

Etti Summers is the author of wonderfully romantic fiction with happy ever afters guaranteed.

She is also a wife, a mum, a pink gin enthusiast, a veggie grower and a keen reader.

Printed in Great Britain
by Amazon

39258546R00182